A Golden Realm

Published by CompletelyNovel.com

First published in the UK in 2016 by Completely Novel.

ISBN 978-1-84914-987-7

Acknowledgements

A massive amount of appreciation to Margaret Dunman whose encouragement, support and active help is responsible for the presence of this book!

Likewise, enormous thanks to Tony Bowles who designed the front cover, just as I envisaged it, and for all the hard work and experience required to bring my novel to fruition.

Author's Note

It started in the war!

I was already an evacuee in Ely Cambridgeshire attending the village school when the Jewish Free School suddenly descended upon us from London. As the only Jewish evacuee in town I quickly moved over to the JFS and thereafter enjoyed the happiest school days of my life! The main reason was the need for eye drops which made it impossible to participate in lessons, and so I sat at the back of the room concocting stories in my head. These I finally shared with classmates to eventually put them on paper. And thus my desire to write took root.

War over and back to London the time eventually arrived to look for a job preferably in a publishing company, I should be so lucky! But I did make it to Fleet Street working in the News Chronicle, alas not as a writer, but typing and proof reading knitting patterns and football results, a soul destroying job!

Thereafter I worked in a whole variety of businesses including Drapers Record and the Yorkshire Post but it was my last position in a Wardour Street film company that my dreams were realised and I found my destiny............

Kitty K. Arscott

Dedicated to my very precious family and friends, past and present.

Golden Realm.

Oh Belle, you'll be the death of me!
What's all this about leaving Dovoud?
You've only just married him! Wish to
heaven you'd married a Frenchman
instead of a Persian, then I could at
least have met you in Paris for a heart
to heart. Of course Dovoud isn't sorry
he married you! If he's touchy it's
because he suddenly has such a lot on
his plate. For goodness sake remember
that last year he was just a light
hearted student having a whale of a
time over here. Now he's back in his
own country, a working man and a
married one at that … I guess the
change takes some getting used to!
        Now be sensible and turn the other
cheek and give him an extra dose of
schmoozing, he'll soon unwind then,
just you see. Anyway if a few sharp
words are all you have to put up with
count yourself lucky. You can't look at
the News Chronicle these days without
reading about a husband who's beaten
the livin' daylights out of his missus
or indulged in peculiar sexual
activities! And talking of sex Nadia's
at it again, languishing over an
Israeli this time. He's having a couple
of pals up to his flat in Finchley this
weekend and wants Nad to bring me
along. I suppose I sound like a wet

blanket but I've neither the time nor inclination for the sort of evening it's bound to be!

I don't know, all you girls with your foreign boyfriends and me hankering after someone who couldn't be more English. Do you realize I've been working for Mark for eighteen months and he's just condescended to call me Marilyn instead of Miss Ash.

At the mo I'm surrounded by stills for "The Naked Tongue" which is having a P.R. next month; all the stars and bosses will be there. Haven't decided what I'll wear (not that Mark would notice if I turned up in my birthday suit for all the interest he has in me). Take yesterday for example, I had a splitting headache and everyone said I looked green but did Mark notice? Not on your life. His only concern was that his precious work should be up to date.

Yet he can be so kind. Remember how generous he was when Billy's mum was in hospital? Not only did he give Billy afternoons off for visiting, but cash to cover fare and flowers. I'd like to see another employer bother half as much over a mere errand boy. I reckon it was his kindness which made me aware of him as a person rather than just a reasonable, pleasant boss.

Is it hot over there? At last we've some good weather and last weekend I was at Valley View in shorts and bra most of the time. You know

nearly all the crowd there - Sonny
Tauber, fat as ever but fun, Judy
Fisher etc. they all send their love.
There were only two strangers in the
camp. One was a Johnny Margolis who
turned out to be quite a boy, gorgeous
brown eyes for a start and y'know what
a sucker I am for brown eyes. The other
chap wasn't much cop. A load of us
walked to the pub for cider and crisps.
Big Sister was with Stan, a Pole, and
after a while this Johnny sidles over
to me.

"Think I'd better keep an eye on
you", he announces, "Looks as if you've
had a couple of crisps too many!"
(ouch).

Connie didn't look too happy and
while we spent a penny she warned,
"Just keep your wits about you Lyn,
that boy has a reputation." As if I
hadn't guessed. But Johnny behaved like
a mensch for most of the time.

We had a lovely evening back in
Camp. The boys made a fire and we sat
round listening to Sinatra and Mel
Torme. Someone had already collared the
sofa so Johnny and I brought blankets
from his bunk to stick on the floor
(that's when he tried his damnest - in
the dorm). Connie looked frightfully
worried when we arrived back. Amazing
isn't it, how it's ok for her to let
her hair down but I have to behave
myself! Not that I'd want to do
otherwise with just anyone. The music

and firelight were marvellous and all the time I pretended Johnny was Mark.

Connie told me Johnny used to go with one of the girls in her gown shop and his dad owns a couple of electrical firms in the West End, but Johnny himself is "on the knowledge" − learning to be a taxi driver. Which reminds me of cousin Sam. Remember him at our house one Pesach? Well when he isn't driving his cab, Sam's going with a girl called Freda who isn't Jewish and this is making the family sick with worry. Quite honestly I don't know who to shout for because I certainly don't want Auntie Rita and Uncle Al hurt, on the other hand I don't want Sam to be unhappy. I had a crush on him once but that finished when I heard you can't marry first cousins!

Funny isn't it, before I met Mark I was as bad as everyone else about intermarriage. The thought of going out with a non-Jew never crossed my mind. Well, would it yours? Do they have such things as Youth Clubs in Persia or places like Valley View where the young can get together? The Shah's a good looking chap isn't he and he seems to be a decent ruler.

Must tell you − walked down Wardour Street with your successor and is she a drip! Ladders in her stockings, hair a right mess. I don't know how Mr Goodman stands her. I still get an awfully queer feeling when I go to Contracts and find you missing.

Oh lor, here's Mark back from lunch, so I must finish. Now take hold of yourself dear Belle, be more tolerant of Dovoud ok? After all, you have the man you want so count your blessings and spare a thought for those who harbour an unrequited love – like me! Love to you both and write soon to tell me all is under control.   Lyn.

Pal, I'm so bursting you must drop everything and listen!

I've been out with Mark — alone! This morning we had the P.R. for "The Naked Tongue" (rotten film) at the Piccadilly. Usual smoked salmon tidily-bits and champ going the rounds. The old crowd were there, Directors, Producers, starlets all hob-nobbing with the Press boys and little me in charge of Stills, doing a good job as always quietly and efficiently???? When a rather luscious chap from a Daily brought me a drink and suggested we went through the Stills together away from the maddening crowd! Of course he was only joking, but Mark was nearby and overheard and told the bloke to get what he wanted and move on!

Can you imagine how I felt? Must have gone as red as a beetroot; fortunately the chap didn't mind because he winked and obediently disappeared. Mark then turned to me and said coldly, "It's certainly essential for you to co-operate with the Press, Marilyn, but there's no need to go to the extreme." What cheek — the pompous ass!

If I'd the pluck I'd have stalked out of the hotel there and then. What right had he to tell me how to conduct myself! Oh, I was livid.

The Press eventually left rosy and mellow to write up their normal biting and shattering reviews and I began to pack up. Dickie helped and suddenly demanded to know why I'd such a long face. Wasn't any point in telling him, so made out I had a headache whereupon the dear boy offered to take everything back to the office so I could go off tout-suite for food and rest.

The thing is Belle, after a penny well spent and a quick splash in the powder room, I returned to the foyer to find Mark standing there – and I'd thought he'd left ages ago. I don't have to tell you how my heart was thumping. I might be livid with him but that didn't stop me loving him.

I'm going to lunch now, Mr Butler," says I primly preparing to march past.

And he says (wait for it), "How about us having lunch together?"

How I contained myself I'll never know; in fact I wanted to spend another penny from the shock! I was certain he must see my excitement in my eyes if not on my soppy face.

We went to a restaurant not far from the hotel, but don't ask me where. The state I was in it could have been Timbuktu and I'd be none the wiser. Anyway I chose a simple steak and chips and oi vey you should have seen that steak when it appeared – blood oozing all over the plate, obviously hadn't been koshered! Of course I pretended it was fine but let me tell you I hadn't been here in the office for very long before it all came up!

I'd loved to have asked Mark about himself but didn't have the nerve. But I did find out that he's lived in Richmond for a long time and even has a house of his own and a daily woman to see to things, which puts paid to the dirty talk here. Y'know Barbie's mind. She's told all and sundry Mark's like that! Mind you, shan't be satisfied until I know why he hasn't got hitched. He should have been snapped up years ago – he's so delish. But then perhaps he has been married and got divorced or lost his wife. Gosh it hurts to think of him belonging to someone else. How old would you say he is? Twenty-eight, thirty, older even?

Of course when we didn't talk I got into a panic wondering if he was bored. Certainly the meal hadn't left him very mellow 'cause we hadn't been back here more than a couple of minutes than he was dictating letter after letter until I could have thrown my book at him! At the mo he's in with Creeping Jesus, that's why I'm able to write this.

Not long had a letter from Maurice asking whether I'll go out with him when he comes home from B'ham. The last time we had a date he was too handy and I lost my temper. He was sorry of course because he really seems to care for me – too bad, he leaves me absolutely stone cold! Why I wonder when he's so good looking and charming with it. Any other girl would grab him with open arms yet I just can't get worked up. Maurice says I'm frigid and ought to do something about it before I get much older! I know this isn't true … why I only have to look at Mark and I get funny feelings simply everywhere!

Needless to say pal, glad to hear all's well between that passionate Persian and yourself, not that I thought anything would come of your tiff. After all you two went through to stay together you must love each other to distraction. Not everyone tries to commit suicide to get their way! Never in a thousand years will I forget your In-Laws' cable arriving and the frantic race to get a visa and that mad mad farewell party and the send-off at the airport. Seems like a dream now, but it was more like a nightmare then wasn't it?

How d'you spend your weekends – with the In-Laws or out and about with Dovoud? Where is there to go in Tehran for a break? I'll probably spend the weekend with Nadia (heaven help me). Last time I was there Philip and young Martin had a real stinker of a row. Martin had invited a school pal for Friday evening and Philip more or less said he didn't want any yoks hanging around, especially on Shabbas. My stomach turned right over but Martin kept his temper. I could hardly bring myself to speak to Phil afterwards, wonder what his reaction would be if he knew how I felt about a certain goy.

Don't look now chum but Fanny Adams is coming my way, so must go. Cheerio, God bless.

Lyn.

Le Boudoir – or is it La?

Dearest Norma,

Hi and about time too! I thought you'd forgotten me. It's
been so long since you last wrote. And guess where I read
your letter this morning? No, not in the loo or in the train
to town, but right here in bed and it's not Sunday either!
You see there I was three days ago, walking down the
stairs at work in the most orderly fashion, when for no
reason at all I take a tumble and plunge to the bottom. I
must have given an almighty yell because everyone came
running including darling Mark! He and our Charmer gave
me a chairlift back to the office while Sally rang for a taxi
to whip me up to the Casualty dept.

We were at the hospital for ages and I was x-rayed
and prodded all over by a rather gorgeous looking doctor,
but nothing was broken just badly bruised. Doc said I was
to rest up for at least a week so here I am. Ages ago I'd
have been overjoyed at being laid off work but with Mark
at the office I'm hating every minute of being away. I
couldn't protest because Creeping Jesus saw that I was put
in a taxi and brought home at the firm's expense; I think
he must be worried in case I sue for damages.

I'm bored stiff! Mummy brings home magazines –
she wanted to stay home from the shop but I said there
wasn't any need – and Sylvie's a darling coming across to
make me elevenses and lunch. So lucky to have such
fantastic neighbours but mustn't forget she expects me to
end up with her brovver! Not a hope! All I can think of is
being back with Mark and wondering if he's missing me!
Don't think so because Sal phoned to find out how I was
and there wasn't any message from him. Not even a query
about the work I was doing before the fall.

Mind you there was one good thing about the accident. I was that close to Mark while he was carrying me back to the office I could have brushed my cheek against his – if I'd had the pluck.

Glad I didn't have the fall a couple of weeks ago 'cause there was cousin Shirley's twenty-first. I bought her a Count Basie record and Mum bought a housecoat. What a party! Must have been over thirty of us noshing and dancing all over the house. Connie was there of course (worse luck) and she took her current boyfriend Stan, and I invited Johnny Margolis along: I met him at Valley View and we get along fine – when he behaves! Last time you saw Shirl she was blonde remember? Now she's gone red, think it would suit me? I had an inkling she wasn't as happy as she ought to be on such a momentous occasion and during the night persuaded her to have a good old heart to heart in the bathroom.

You'll never believe this, Norm, but she's fallen hook, line and sinker in love with a Rabbi of all people! But not a bearded old crony like our Rabbi Silberman. Her boyfriend's an American Liberal Minister who's been at her Synagogue for nearly a year and a half although she's only got to know him well during the last eight months. She says she can kick herself for wasting so much time!

There's no girl back in the States to make things difficult for them, it's just that Shirl can't bear the thought of leaving Auntie Yetta if she married Paul – yes it's gone as far as that! At the same time she can't stand the thought of losing Paul who's scheduled to go home pretty soon. I suggested Auntie Yetta goes with them, she's young enough to start life in a new country, but Shirley doesn't think her mum would leave Ivor behind.

Poor Auntie, she's had a raw deal with Uncle Ben dropping dead so suddenly and then Solly going off to Canada and not bothering to keep in touch. How can a son be so cruel? And Ivor isn't really pulling his weight. Do you know what he's doing now? He's in the market selling ladies underwear! I know he's earning a bomb, but what a waste of all that good education that Auntie and Uncle slaved to give him. My Mum and Dad don't know how well off they are to have such uncomplicated daughters as Connie and myself!

Just after six in the morning, Shirley, Con and me were frying eggs and bread for breakfast and by ten everyone at the party had cleared off and Auntie suggested that the three of us went back to bed 'til lunch. She's a real sport. Funny isn't it how she wouldn't dream of us merry making on a Friday evening because it's Shabbas, but the thought of us spending Saturday night in the arms of a strong young man doesn't trouble her. Ah well, that's trust for you.

Hope this tookus and back of mine doesn't trouble me on holiday. We're going to hitchhike from Paris to the South of France – actual destination as yet unknown. I'm going with Connie and Fay, a friend of Con's who's hitched before. Wanted Nadia to come along but her boss is being difficult and won't spare her. The only thing casting a shadow over the coming holiday is the thought of being away from Mark again. Yes pal, I really do like him as much as ever!

Simply must write to Maurice. Ages since I had his last letter. It was sweet of him to bother about me really; Sylvie says he's absolutely enveloped in exams. Anyway I intend to put my cards on the table and tell him that I find him attractive and good company (not true) but I've no intention of entering into anything permanent and if he doesn't like it, well he knows what he can do!

What a lucky so and so you are to be able to listen to music out in the open air under the stars. At this very mo I'm listening to an organ recital, not too keen but there are moments of great beauty, which make it worthwhile. Just as well Dad isn't around to hear. When he heard me listening to a Bach Mass recently he went off his rocker. He doesn't understand I hear it as <u>music</u> and not in relation to Christianity.

Incidentally, Shirley's rabbi hails from Baltimore, how far away is that from Houston? Are you still infatuated with the States or ready to come home! Oh I wish you would! I do miss you and Belle. It was bad enough when Belle went off to her Dovoud, but when your family decided out of the blue to try their luck abroad, that was the end. It's not very often that a girl loses her two "sisters" all in one year. And we were like sisters weren't we? Oh I know I've got Nadia still and thank heavens for that, but I'm greedy. I want you and Belle too!

Belle's letters are very inconsistent: one minute everything's glorious and the next she's down in the dumps. Mind you it must be absolutely ghastly not having anyone to talk to. None of her In-Laws speak English and Dovoud's at work all day. She's talking about finding herself a job before she goes mashigah. I always send her your love and she sends hers to you. Shame you're both such lousy letter writers or you could exchange regards in person. Just as well I don't mind scribbling <u>and waiting</u> for your replies or I'd never know what the two of you were up to!

And hey, next time you write please enlarge on your friendship with this Irvine. It hasn't gone unnoticed that your letter before last was full of "Irvine does this" and "Irvine does that". So spill the beans or else!

Sylvie's just looked in to say it's time to rest and have I written to her brother yet! Take care of yourself and write soon.

Love, Lyn.

What can I say to cheer you up, dear
Belle? Although what you really need is
a good shake! You're just looking for
trouble when you think Dovoud has his
eye on this Mahi girl. He just isn't
the sort to mess around. Mind you if
you carry on nagging him and spending
nights on the couch instead of in his
bed, you'll probably send him right
into Mahi's arms and then you'll
certainly have something to moan about!

Pal, can't you get it through that
thick skull of yours, Dovoud knew <u>who</u>
and <u>what</u> he was passing over when he
chose to marry <u>you</u>? After all, he and
this girl had been "betrothed" since he
was in nappies – well almost! And he
knew all about her virtues and
attractions before coming over here,
yet when he returned to Tehran it
<u>wasn't</u> Mahi he wanted for a wife was
it? He braved his family's wrath and
disapproval by sticking out for <u>you</u> by
taking an overdose! Not going to let a
petty incident upset things surely? No
one except yourself can prove to Dovoud
and his family that he made the right
choice …

Have I got through to you yet? Now
as soon as you've read this letter I
want you to be a big girl and make
yourself lovely for Dovoud. It won't

take a lot of doing because you're naturally beautiful, but put on some extra perfume and your prettiest dress or, if it's night time, your most stunning nightie - all the better! Don't think I'm taking this commotion too lightly, I really do know what it's like to be jealous. I get sick with jealousy every time Mark as much as looks at another woman, even Fanny Adams who I know he wouldn't touch with a barge pole!

And while we're on the subject of Mark! Let me tell you how things are going in this part of the world, and seeing you're so full of woe I feel a little guilty at my own joy 'cause everything is progressing wonderfully well between us. Take the firm's outing for instance - and to think I wasn't going because of the longish journey but the weather's been so fantastically marvellous for this time of year that Mum said the sea air would do me good.

The coach was full to bursting and Mark sat down front with the other Exe, while I travelled with our mob, but when the coach made one of its stops for a drink Mark sat at a table with me! Oh I know Sally, Dickie, Barbie and others were with us, but it was me he asked if I was enjoying the ride. I wondered what we'd do when we arrived at Bognor; where would Mark go and should I have to hang around with the girls? Tables had been booked for lunch at a rather swell hotel and might have been okay except Mark was at the far end of the dining room with the other bosses.

Afterwards the girls wanted to go on the Pier but I said I preferred to find a deckchair and doze in the sea air. Won't deny I raised my voice in the hope Mark would hear and perhaps be interested! I'd just about got settled in a deckchair when WHO strolls up? Incredible as it might sound, Mark! He said he'd no wish to traipse round the town and he might as well sit with me as anyone …

We didn't have much to say to one another really, he read his paper and I closed my eyes and basked in his being near. I'm sure he must have heard my heart thumping away. He was wearing flannels, a creamy shirt and navy blazer and looking so gorgeous and approachable. I wonder what he thought of me? I told him I was lucky to be able to go to the seaside whenever I wanted throughout the year, having relations in Brighton. He said Brighton was his favourite English resort and he often took a quick drive down there over the weekend which set me daydreaming about meeting him down there in the future!

About tea-time it became nippy and Mark suggested a drink so we found a cute place, very olde worlde, with scones, jam and cream with our pot of tea. I was "mother" pouring more tea into the saucers than cups because I was so nervous, and ended up feeling thoroughly sick, a combination of excitement and too much cream I reckon.

Afterwards we took a slow stroll back along the Prom and eventually returned to the hotel to meet the others. Dickie gave us a rather strange look when we arrived together! I wouldn't be surprised if he didn't fancy Mark himself! He's got a smashing face you know (Mark), not Van Johnsonish mind you, who I adore, but definitely appealing. A very firm chin, grey eyes (Yes I've deserted brown ones!) and oooh his mouth! Now Maurice is really handsome but there's something definitely lacking. When I look at Mark my heart goes topsy-turvy!

We hadn't been on the road for more than ten minutes when I began to feel sick and by the time we'd stopped at our second pub all I wanted to do was die! Mark was most concerned and insisted I came into the Saloon bar with him and have some soda while the mass went into the Public Saloon. It was almost worth feeling ill to have him so sweet! I pretended to be better by the time we returned to the coach but I was actually dreading the rest of the journey. Well you know what those journeys are like Belle. Fumes of the coach, fumes from the crowd who'd hogged beer and cider; cigarette smoke and oh the noise, bedlam! But I could hardly have expected anything else. "Ten Green Bottles" etc is all part of an outing.

The only good thing which came out of the journey home was Mark coming to sit next to me, and now and again ordering everyone to lower their voices but no one seemed particularly worried about his watchful eye, they were all too far gone. Billy had drunk far too much for his own good and was flirting like mad with a junior from London Branch. The Charmer wasn't doing too badly either in the back seat with a girl from Contracts. Not seen her before, she must be new. I must have dozed off because when I came to it was to find myself leaning against Mark's shoulder; he didn't seem to mind and was very relieved when I was well enough to get down from the coach unaided – unlike our Billy and one or two others who were drunk. I wasn't able to say goodnight to Mark 'cause he was busy putting Billy and others in taxis, and Sal whipped me off to catch the train.

All Sunday I was on top of the world thinking how he'd seemed to single me out, but come Monday I was soon brought down to earth. D'you know he worked me almost to death and has been wretched to me ever since. I simply haven't been able to do a thing right in his eyes; true we've all been run off our feet with trade shows and new Campaign books but I honestly can't see why he's had to be so sharp with me. I've been in tears more than once and Mummy's so fed up she threatens to write and tell "Mr Butler" I'm being overworked!

And then, TODAY, not more than an hour ago, he stuns me completely by saying there's a Concert at the weekend with a marvellous programme and, "Would you care to enjoy it with me?"

Would I????? So I'm sitting here typing this letter, hardly able to sit still for the joy bubbling inside me! Just what do I make of this heavenly man? Is it possible he's beginning to be interested in me and, if so, why? Oh Belle, how I wish .. but I'm being foolish to get so excited. I haven't decided (a) what to wear (b) when to have my hair done and (c) what to tell Mummy because I don't think she'll be too happy at my going out with (a) my boss and (b) a non-Jew!

Mind you, she met him for a brief second (remember Premiere at the Carlton "From Dawn to Dusk"?) and she was favourably impressed "A nice looking man", but not, I should imagine, to the extent of sanctioning a date with him. A DATE!

You see, I'm in a whirl just like yourself only for a very different reason, but do as I've told you chum and everything'll be fine. Remember

Dovoud didn't choose Mahi in the beginning even, she was selected by his parents. <u>You</u> are Dovoud's own personal choice and I know he wouldn't change you for the Queen of Persia even! Kiss him for me and write soon,

God bless,

Lyn

Home.

Didn't post the enclosed letter after all! Thought I'd wait
until the big event had come and gone so I could tell you
all about it. Everything was wonderful, Mark and the
music.

Needless to say I couldn't sleep a wink on Friday
night and woke with such a bilious attack that Mummy
threatened to stay home and nurse me! Thank goodness I
reassured her that a rest and pills would put me right and
hooray they did the trick. Mind you by the time I was
ready to travel my hair looked as if it hadn't been touched
and I felt thoroughly washed out. Several times during the
journey I nearly got off the train – I was so scared at the
thought of going out with Mark alone – alone! Anyway, I
eventually reached Charing X and, oh lor, it had started to
rain quite heavily and all I was wearing was a white suit
(boucle wool, navy blouse bought C & A) and skimpy
high heels. Yes I know, should have dressed more sensibly
but I didn't want to be cluttered up. I don't think Mark
was too thrilled with me 'cause we had to hang around in
the station for a while 'til the rain lessened and then we
made a quick dash to a restaurant for a meal.

It was hot in there and what with being nervous I
could feel myself getting all sweaty and jolly
uncomfortable but I didn't dare take off my jacket in case
I was wet under the arms. Mark looked wonderful; he was
wearing grey for a change. At the office he keeps to navy
which suits him too of course but is on the sober side. Oh
Belle, I do so adore him! He was absolutely charming and
when he lets himself go, quite fun! We talked about other
concerts and shows, he wanted to know what I liked best. I
can hardly believe my luck, we both enjoy the big bands

like Ted Heath, he enjoys Sinatra, and of course the classics. For some of the time I managed not to feel dithery while we were talking, but then suddenly I'd find myself looking right into his eyes and – whoops!

Can you remember what it was that first made you notice Dovoud? Mark's so smart. I love his hands; his nails are always nicely shaped and clean. Maurice's fingers make me shudder, they're rather hairy and he bites his nails dreadfully.

As I said before the music lived up to expectation. You would have enjoyed it. First there was "Don Juan" and then Chopin, some real gems. During the interval I had tomato juice and went to "powder my nose". Always embarrassing when you want to spend a penny! You should have seen my reflection; talk about stars in my eyes. Hard to believe he couldn't see how I felt about him! And during the Beethoven I absolutely ached to put my hand in his …..

I'd hoped he would suggest coffee after the concert but it was getting late and he thought I'd better make a move for home, and promptly took me to the station, saying casually before the train whisked me away, "I'll see you on Monday, Lyn." LYN!

I grinned and glowed from that moment on, and the way in which he'd said my name – not stuffy Marilyn as usual but Lyn, echoed in my ears throughout the journey. I wouldn't be surprised if my fellow passengers didn't think they were travelling with a loony, but I just couldn't wipe the smile off my face!

So now you know! But the way Mark's behaved to me today is another matter entirely. Oh he did condescend to ask if I'd arrived home all right, but that's all. No discussion about our outing together, no smile or friendly word. I'm now listening to Sinatra and feeling weepy.

Better finish and tuck down; Connie's just come in from a dance and she'll probably put her nose round the door to see if I'm awake to hear the latest developments in her sordid love life!

Once again, love to Dovoud, chin up,

Lyn.

Dearest Maurice,

Just a brief note to say sorry I wasn't able to see you during your lightning visit but I was busy. Sylvie told me all about the banger and glad you've managed to buy it but do take it easy when you're behind that wheel. If anything happened to you it would kill Sylvie!

On Saturday went to the theatre with Nad and Joyce, a girl from British Lion. We saw "The Same Sky" with Yvonne Mitchell who also wrote it. Very good and thought provoking, what a clever woman Yvonne Mitchell is to be able to both write and act as well.

On Sunday went out with Nadia again and some South African cousins of hers. Went to Lyons Corner Hse for a meal and thoroughly enjoyed ourselves. They live in Johannesburg and are very well off. They've a rambling house, acres of property and little black boys to do their bidding. I wonder what they thought of the Samuels titchy home in the East End?

Surprised to hear from Sylv that you're going to Switzerland for the Christmas hols. Where will you hang your Chanukah stocking? And you aren't going in that car are you????? For heavens sake be careful up on those there mountains! Connie's by my side and says some people have all the luck, she's always wanted to go abroad for winter sports. Not me, it's not my idea of fun, quite bad enough when I have to slosh my way along snow-covered pavements up West to get to work.

Bye for now, happy times and be careful!

Lyn

Thanks a heap dear Norm for your birthday card, it's really pretty and fantastic that it arrived right on time! Mum and Dad have given me a fiver to spend on something sensible, and Nad took me out for a meal at the weekend. We were determined to stand clear of the Salad Bowl even tho' the idea of being able to pile up our plate as many times as we wanted was tempting. So we made for a Chinese restaurant and the p-k Sweet and Sour was sinful but delicious! Afterwards we went window shopping and Nadia saw a rather gorgeous black cocktail dress and plans to try it on after work today. She's going to her Shul's Chanukah Ball and want me to go with her but as it's two quid a ticket I'm going to think about it!

Glad to hear about your job's still okay and that your new flat mate is helpful. Mark told me some time ago that when he first left home he shared a flat with three other chaps and it was a riot. Most important to get on with everyone if you want to be happy; Connie talks about getting a flat if Dad doesn't stop nagging her about lights and noise (she has her radio on loud enough for the whole neighbourhood to hear!) and I pity the poor people who get her to share!

Nadia and her Israeli are as close as ever. What's he like? Swarthy and handsome. I've a sort of love-hate relationship with him; I like him because he appreciates good music and comes from the Promised Land, but I resent him because he takes up so much of Nadia's time and thoughts. In fact if I'm quite frank with you, I'm as jealous as hell when Isadore comes to the Samuel's while I'm there so that I have to share Nadia's company with him. I'm glad he's fond of her of course, but at the same time I'm terrified he might get it into his head to whip her back to Israel and then I don't know what I'll do.

The Samuel family think there's no one quite like Isadore, who brings Mrs S. little gifts and listens with deference to Mr Samuel's political opinions. As for young Martin he loves to hear Isadore chat about Israel and I am sure as soon as he had a chance he'll be out there like a shot whether dad likes it or not. But then perhaps I haven't told you about the trouble brewing between Martin and his dad?

One weekend when I was staying with them Martin said his Headmaster had arranged for him to talk with the Careers Officer. Mr Samuel was livid and said it wasn't anybody's business what Martin was going to do when he leaves school next year – anyway his future was already worked out. But

Martin wasn't having any of that and told his dad as much.

"I'd rather be dead than spend my life making schmattes in a stuffy old workshop!"

I thought Mr Samuel was going to have a stroke! His face went scarlet and all his veins bulged. You can understand him being upset because Martin's the only one left to carry on his business. David's in accountancy, Phil's in window display; Sylvie and Nadia refused to go anywhere near a sewing machine, and Yetta worked at the factory for only a few months before she married and started a family – and she hasn't stopped production yet! She's twenty six and has three kids already and now expects another one. I know it's supposed to be a mitzvah to have a big family but this is overdoing it, don't you think?

Well Martin and his dad'll have to sort it out between themselves and I wish them both the best of British Luck because I don't think either one will give in.

Now let me tell you a little about our Belle. In her last letter she said she thought Dovoud was straying! Her In-Laws had a "supper" for friends and invited Mahi along, she's the girl Dovoud was engaged to before coming over here. You know how they arrange schidachs out there almost as soon as the children can sit up and take notice!

Apparently Dovoud was most charming to Mahi, more charming than Belle thinks he had any need to be! Further more, he invited Mahi up to their flat for a drink the following week without first consulting Belle – this really started the fireworks. I've written telling her she's making a mountain out of a molehill and to stop being a twerp. I haven't heard since so either all's well or she isn't satisfied with my advice!

Made friends with a girl in British Lion. She's quite a character and Nadia likes her. Sometimes we meet for a roll and coffee in the Film Cafe; recently the three of us went to see "The Same Sky". It was very good, about a Jewish girl falling in love with a non-Jewish boy wouldn't you know, and all the heartache that befalls them and their families and he eventually gets killed during the war. Joyce (British Lion) said the story was good but she really couldn't see what all the fuss was about!

Joyce is a very dedicated film-goer, thinks her firm's films are the best of course! She's got this almost obsessive admiration for Anna Neagle and Herbert Wilcox who are two of B.L's biggest stars, and she even says she's on talking terms with them. I think she's a bit of a story-teller herself!

But she is very loyal to them, travelling all over the country to be at first nights of their films, and see them when they're making a Personal Appearance. I thought Anna Neagle and Michael Wilding made a smashing pair in "Piccadilly Incident" and "Spring in Park Lane". I wish we made such films instead of the dull stuff we do turn out.

Life's been jolly hectic here one way and another. Take the week we premièred "The Trouble With Love" and on the actual day of the Première everything went haywire the moment we set foot in the office. The Chief-on-High had decided to send out more personal invitations than Creeping Jesus had allowed for, and we weren't sure there'd be enough seats, so Mark (no less obnoxious than everyone else that day!) and I had to keep 'phoning people to find out whether they were actually going to use their ticket. Then Sal and I had to type out fresh guest lists for the press, while Billy rushed round London in a taxi collecting spare tickets and taking them to where they were needed most. Billy was the only one having fun!

Next catastrophe was Fanny Adam's cocktail dress which she'd taken to the cleaners at the bottom of the street. When Barbie brought it back, F.A. nearly hit the roof because it had shrunk so much. You can imagine what a

foul mood she was in after this! Thank
goodness there's the Hire shop along
the road, they eventually sorted her
out and she ended up with a dress
better than her own!

We had our lunchtime shortened
because there was so much to do and I
was furious because I'd had a hair
appointment which I had to cancel. And
that wasn't my only trouble by far.
Listen to this. Getting ready for the
evening we had to wash in freezing cold
water and I went almost frantic because
my fringe wouldn't lie down properly,
and then to crown it all I took my
lenses out to put in fresh liquid and
when it came to putting 'em back, put a
lens in the wrong eye and couldn't get
it out again. Something I've not done
since I've had them. What a panic! I
had the girls in stitches and I didn't
know whether to laugh or cry myself.

What was worse I hadn't brought my
plunger to work, and as if all that
wasn't enough, Mark barges in to say he
can hear the noise from the end of the
passage and what on earth's going on? I
thought he'd already gone to the
theatre and was horrified at the idea
of him seeing me with my fringe on end
and only one eye in, and the wrong one
at that! I warned the girls I'd murder
them if they said anything to him and
rushed into the office, stuck a chair
against the door so he couldn't get in
if he wanted to and tried frantically

to get the damn lens out. At last success but I was in such a state the girls told me to leave myself alone until I got to the theatre. So the four of us finally trotted off together, me holding on to Sal and Billy for dear life because y'know how blind I am without my lenses and of course I hadn't thought to bring any specs.

The usual mob were outside the theatre. Guests, passers-by cramming to see the stars; barmy fans, police and, as usual, Mark and our Charmer somewhere in the middle of the foyer organizing everything while C.J. flapped around. How I adore the thrill of a first night! Incidentally I wore a blue lurex cocktail dress I bought for a cousin's barmitzvah. Sleeveless, very slim fitting in the new maxi length, high roll-neck collar, and I borrowed a brooch from Connie to finish it off only she doesn't know! Of course Mark hasn't had reason to see me in the dress and I was hoping to bowl him over, but we never caught a glimpse of each other because - and you'll never believe this - when I went to the loo to tidy myself up, I found I'd left my lenses back at the office!

I could have screamed! Well there wasn't any point in me hanging around because I couldn't see the screen even if I was stuck in the orchestra pit, so there was nothing to do but go home. When I arrived home it was to find Mum in an absolute flap, Mark having just phoned to ask if I was with her! Mum naturally told him I was supposed to be at a Première, and Mark explained that I'd momentarily been mislaid! Poor Mum, can you imagine the thoughts which must have flown through her mind. Her innocent little girl abducted in Piccadilly …..

Wasn't until I was safely tucked up in bed that I wondered why Mark should be so concerned about my whereabouts and how he's come to be looking for me in the theatre anyway? Went to sleep hugging my pillow and pretending it was Mark!

Next morning I waited impatiently for him to say something on the subject but not a dickie about his telephone call or my disappearing the night before. But then, just before lunch, he looked up from his work and suggested that as we were going to a trade show later, we might as well have a snack together first!

It was only the Film Café this time but who cares. He told me how worried everyone had been when my seat remained empty at the Premiere and I couldn't be found. He got Billy and Dickie and a few others looking for me! I thanked him for his concern and assured him I was quite capable of looking after myself, whereupon he gave me the most marvellous smile and said, "Sometimes I wonder!"

I could have been imagining things I know dear Norma, but at that moment I felt we were very close. Yes, that's the word, <u>close</u>. But the feeling hasn't lasted, oh dear me no, there he is at this very moment, remote and business-like at his desk and here I am at mine longing for him.

Heavens haven't I gone on; hope I haven't been a bore. At least you know I think of Belle and yourself a great deal and look forward eagerly to receiving your letters. Thanks again for the card, and let me know your plans and how you intend to spend the Christmas hols over there.

I'd really better get on with some work now or I'll get my cards. Not that I'd miss the cash believe me, but I couldn't do without Mark!

God bless,

Lyn

Just as well you can't see me pal; I'm looking like some monster from outer space! I'm all beady-eyed and my nose is shining like a Belisha beacon, all because I've been crying up here in my bedroom … you see we've broken up for Christmas hols which means five whole days away from Mark. Oh Belle, an eternity!

What's worse is that he's spending the holiday in a Brighton hotel with friends – including Valerie Cripps. Now I don't kid myself that Mark's any less human than the next man, and I can just imagine what he'll get up to during the festivities. There'll be drinks and mistletoe. And Valerie! I'm simply aching with jealousy and frustration.

I'll be going out myself but my heart won't be in it. I'm fed up with Nadia who's bought tickets for a Club dance and asked Isadore to bring one of his cronies for me. I wouldn't go only Dad heard her tell me about the ticket and when I started to make excuses, he blew up and called me stick in the mud, so if I did stay home he'd give me no peace.

What will you two be doing with yourselves? And what have you bought Dovoud for Chanukah? I've bought Nadia a marvellous white sweater. I think she's bought me a red one, and we're bound to borrow each others at some point or other. I've got Connie a rather posh photo frame for her current pin-up boy, Stanislav, Mummy a cardigan and talc, Daddy a pullover and cigars. I've bought Sylvie a Sinatra record (which I hope to borrow), Jon-Jon some toys and Maurice I'm still getting! Sylvie says he's bought me a Jacqmar scarf which is very generous of him seeing I treat him so rotten.

Before I left the office today I gave Mark a lovely thick book on sailing because I know he goes on his friends yacht whenever he can. He gave me a record token for seventeen and sixpence and signed it <u>Sincerely Mark A. Butler</u>. Don't laugh but the token's under my pillow! I don't know what the A. stands for, any ideas? Alan, Alexander, Armand, Aldo? Alfred, Angus, Adrian, Abraham? Arnold, Archibald, Ashley, Asqith, Arthur, Andronicus! No, none of those names suit him.

I've already written out a list of all the records I want but it's going to take some time before I make a decision. Might get some Sinatra records (and leave Sylvie in peace) on the other hand Connie scratched my favourite Tchaikovsky when she snatched it off to put on her Mel Torme, the slob – Connie not Mel!

And talking about Connie, she's out with her Stan. Mum and Dad aren't very happy about this friendship but really haven't a say in the matter; they can't wind Con around their little fingers like they can me. I think they're silly to fuss because Stan's a sweet chap, too good for the likes of her! She's bossier than ever; at least Stan treats me like an intelligent being and not a half-baked infant as Connie does.

What's your sister-in-law like, you haven't told me anything about her except she can't speak English! I'm jolly glad all's well between Dovoud and yourself and I won't say I told you so! As if he'd be interested in anyone but you, do me a favour! Glad the job's o.k, yes, Mr Goodman does ask after you and always sends his regards.

Mummy's calling me for coffee … what a row downstairs! Ralph's over for a game of cards but he and Daddy are getting worked up about the Government. A fat lot of good their arguing will do! Rail and bus strikes in the air, nurses up in arms, teachers threatening to walk out (pity they didn't do that when I was at school!), dockers already striking. A fine way to start a new year!

By the way I went to a concert with Mark a few weeks ago. Sibelius and it was heavenly and the whole evening wonderful, all the more so because the invitation was unexpected. Our second date! (I must have told you about the time he took me to hear Beethoven at the Royal Albert Hall?)

First we went to an Italian restaurant for a meal and after the concert we had coffee together. Not that we lingered long but at least it was better than being rushed straight to the station. I'm afraid I had to tell darling Mummy a 'story' about the evening: said I was going to a concert with a friend from the office. But when I arrived home, decided to tell her "Saw Mr Butler in the audience" so adding a dash of truth and able to go to bed feeling not quite so dreadful about the deceit.

I owe Norma a letter but that'll have to wait 'til later, best go down before Mum shouts herself hoarse. Let me know how you've spent these hols.

God bless you both,

Lyn

P.S. I'll go and see your Mum and Dad when I go down to Nads and get all the news.

A happy new year Norma - the secular one!

I must say I was thrilled with your snaps; you look as pretty as ever, and Nadia's gone overboard for your Irvine. Such brawn, and I love the crew cut! You're still too cagey about your relationship with him. Nadia says "What goes?" I feel there must be more to tell if you've actually stayed with his family over Christmas. Still I won't be a bore and pry, I'm sure you'll tell me anything important when the right time comes - you'd better! His home and family sound marvellous and if you do get hitched you'll obviously want for nothing. Jolly glad he's Jewish, I couldn't stand any more complication.

We've plenty of trouble brewing right here. Connie's mad keen on her Stanislav, a Pole, and my cousin Sam's got himself married to a C of E! Yes, actually married, on the quiet without anyone but Auntie Rita and Uncle Al and my people knowing. The rest of the family were stunned when news got around and Uncle and Auntie look really grim. Needless to say the Brighton contingent don't want anything to do with Sam any more which hurts his Mum and Dad terribly of course, because Auntie Rita and Auntie Rachel are sisters, and have always been very close.

The four of them came over a week ago in Sam's taxi for supper and although Freda's nothing to write home about she seems perfectly harmless to me and absolutely devoted to Sam which is all that really matters. I don't know if she's going to keep a Jewish home but Sam's used to everything kosher. Of course it'd make things easier if she'd "change" but that's between her and Sam.

As for Connie's Stan, he's a salesman in a men's outfitters up West; I shouldn't think he earns a great deal but it isn't that which irks Dad so much, it's because Stan's Polish, tho I can't make out what's so wrong with that, after all he is Jewish. Anyway Dad really had his eye on Benny across the road for a son-in-law. Benny's a dental surgeon with a posh surgery, have I told you about him? He's quite nice really but Connie's not keen. Benny phoned at Christmas and wanted to take her to a big Charity Ball in town but she wouldn't go. Daddy was livid and said she didn't know what was good for her and if she wasn't careful she'd be left on the shelf. Hardly possible with her good looks, not that I'd tell her she's pretty, it would only make her more big-headed than she already is!

Tonight I am going home with Nadia. We are going to wash each others hair; we're both too broke to go to the hairdressers, and then we'll have a face pack. I'm taking it for granted David and Phil will be out of the house; it'll put them off girls for life if they see us in mud packs and curlers!

Tomorrow we've both got dates. Nad with her Israeli and me with Johnny Margolis, did I ever tell you about him? He's a taxi-driver like Sam and I met him at Valley View. He's great fun but I have to keep my wits about me all the time we're together, if you get what I mean! He and Maurice seem to have only one thing on their minds, but at least Johnny appeals to me.

You'd never recognize this part of the world these days, Norm. So many new businesses springing up. The Cafe on the corner has turned Indian, the hat shop's closed down and there's a rumour we're going to have "educational" books instead - Billy will take longer than ever on his errands! Even "Roberto" is being repainted and had new dryers installed but the customers remain unchanged! Oh gosh, I'll never forget my first week here when I asked Dickie which film companies these dolled-up girls worked for? He just couldn't believe I was that innocent! But have I grown up since then!

Golden Realm's changing too, but not for the better. Not only is there no longer Belle and yourself to brighten things up, but Ossie's left Contracts for another Company, and Tony's been promoted to Ass Branch Manager and become rather toffee-nosed. A shame because he was rather sweet and I must not forget he took me under his wing when I arrived in Wardour St. as inexperienced as a country bumpkin. Can you imagine a worse firm in which to start one's working life? And not only is the pace here still exhausting but the rat race goes on fiercer than ever, everyone trying to outdo the next person. I know Barbie's just aching to step into my shoes but she'll do so over my dead body!

Still I'm glad I persuaded Dad to let me leave school when I did and that the Emp. Agency sent me here or I'd never have met you, Belle or Mark – what a ghastly thought! Mind you I also regret not having worked harder at school and got my matric. Mark's a grammar school boy and sometimes I feel a right dunce (or is it dunse!).

My Christmas doesn't bear thinking about, but from Belle's last letter I gather she had a wow of a time. Apparently while driving to a Boxing Day dance "in the mountains" they saw an Austin Healey on the outside of which was painted "From Birmingham to Sydney"; at first Belle thought it was some publicity stunt but suddenly feeling home sick urged Dovoud to see if the driver was really English. It was all on the level and the B'ham crowd were delighted to meet Belle and, to cut a long story short, they all went to the dance and had a rave up!

Belle found out that the driver was trying to set up a record for A.H. while one of his companions was writing articles about the journey for a daily paper, and hoped later to publish a book on the adventure. What interested me most was the information that the writer's father had been married several times and his latest conquest was none other than the wife of Papa Hemingway! How I love that man's books. I had a token from Sylvie for Chanukah and bought a couple of Penguins.

Dovoud bought Belle a load of fabulous material for her present, and as labour's cheap and plenty out there she's had a couple of outfits run up in no time at all. I think I'll send out my measurements and see what she can do for me! I have bought myself a lime green moygashel suit which I adore but Mummy thinks ghastly! Not quite so easy for Belle to get hold of magazines and knitting patterns - that is, the only patterns available in Teheran are printed in French, I wonder why? Belle would adore some sock patterns, of all things, because she can't buy a pair of woolly socks for love nor money and poor Dovoud's feet are always freezing. Anyway I'm preparing a parcel of patterns and socks – having first phoned Belle's Mum to see if she knows the size of her son-in-law's feet. She's made a wild guess and we'll just have to hope for the best …

And how's my dream-man? He's fine thanks and we're working as hard as ever in the office but he hasn't asked me to any concerts lately or been particularly 'close' … and yet everything was going along just swell before the Christmas hols. Oh I did miss him so much Norma, and could hardly wait to get back here but when I did there was no being met with open arms. He asked me if I'd enjoyed a good Xmas but volunteered no information about his own activities. This is what's worrying me because he spent the hols in a Brighton hotel with friends and Valerie Cripps and she's been with him often recently, too often for my liking.

Perhaps they've come to some understanding and that's why he isn't bothering with me any more. Of course I know, deep down, he can never fall for me, but life's just endurable while I know he isn't attached to anyone else. Damn! When I sat down to write this letter I quite made up my mind not to mention him.

Sally's not too bright at the moment. Did I tell you her Mum and Dad were almost on the brink of splitting up? Apparently Mrs Hudson's going through the 'change' and behaving very queerly … taken a thorough dislike to her husband, accusing him of doing all sorts of things, and Sally assures me her dad is as good as gold. Her Christmas day was a nightmare; they entertained various aunts and uncles and Mrs Hudson behaved dreadfully to Mr H, so that in the end he marched out of the house and didn't come home until early morning. They've pleaded with Mrs Hudson to see a doctor but she says she's perfectly all right thank you and there must be something wrong with them! Poor Sally doesn't know which way to turn. Mummy must be Mrs Hudson's age but she doesn't seem to be having any trouble, mind you I must admit I haven't thought about Mum, or Dad, for that matter, having any emotional feelings or worries, but I suppose they must have.

Must finish now, have tons of stuff to do before home time. Made any new year resolutions? I decided I'd try and be nicer to Connie but that resolution only lasted half an hour! Oh, before I sign off, I must tell you I saw Petula Clark when I was down Berwick Street. She's quite pretty I suppose but no more exciting looking than you and me, but I like her voice and I guess that's what all the fuss is about.

Pardon me, Mark's just come back and is brewing up for dictation; can always tell by the way he rubs that gorgeous chin of his! Love for now and ever, God Bless, Lyn

Hello there dear Belle, such a lot to tell you – and first of all, Connie's engaged! What do you think of that, wonderful isn't it? She and Stan decided out of the blue they're really meant for one another and we're having a simply huge engagement party in a couple of weeks time at a hotel in Kilburn. We've made out an enormous list of relatives and friends and I wouldn't be surprised if this party didn't cost Dad a small fortune.

You'd adore Stan, he's a real chooch, I almost wish he had a brother for me! But it happens that he hasn't anybody except an ancient Uncle. Stan's parents came from Poland, had him here, and died when he was fourteen! He lived with this Uncle until he was old enough to find a place of his own. Poor darling's had a lonely time but now he's got us! Now that Mum and Dad have got used to the idea of Connie marrying him rather than Benny Cohen (he's a dentist and Daddy's choice) they've taken to Stan wholeheartedly. Mum wants to muvver him and Dad wants to give him fatherly advice. Fortunately Stan's the tolerant type (has to be to put up with Connie) and takes it all with a pinch of salt. What's so amusing is that Connie's always gone overboard for the cheesecake type of man and here she is marrying Stan who is as skinny as a bean pole with a thin pale face but lovely kind eyes and he's got a wonderful sense of humour (has to have to put up with Connie!). I know he's going to be an absolutely terrific brother to me.

Nadia and the Samuel tribe will come to the party and Connie says Isadore must come too if it'll make Nadia happy. Who knows perhaps Nad will be the next one to get engaged because Isadore goes back to Israel sometime in the year. Shirley's Rabbi Paul will also be going home, but I can't see any chance of an engagement there because Paul's told Shirley outright he won't take her with him to Georgia – one of the trouble spots in the States. Not that the race problem would worry our Shirl, not even if the KKK put a fiery cross on her own front door – or a fiery Magen David! But it's to Paul's credit I suppose that he's worrying about her safety. We saw them not so long ago and Paul said that if they felt the same way about one another after his contract was up, then he'll come back here to marry her. Two years of separation! A few days, even a few hours, away from Mark is enough to send me mad!

He really is a honey, Rabbi Paul Stern. He can discuss any composer under the sun from Beethoven to Basie. And what he does for our religion is nobody's business. Connie and I went along to hear him take an evening service and for the first time in my life I actually enjoyed rather than put up with the service. Don't worry I'm not getting religious mania! The point is, I could actually take part in the service because a good deal was said in English (with an American accent) and when Hebrew was used it was at a reasonable pace so I could follow. Paul's sermon was all about brotherhood and how we shouldn't be so quick to criticize other people's behavior when our own house needed putting in order. I think he was getting at us because of the fuss in the newspapers about the trouble abroad while we have our own colour problem here.

I wonder how Paul and Shirl behave with one another, physically I mean. After all, Paul may be a Rabbi but he's also a man and you're aware of this even when he's in his Shul outfit. I wonder if his "position" helps him to have more strength and discipline where emotion's concerned or if he's as weak as the next man?

What's it like being married, Belle? Is it too difficult to write about? Perhaps you're shy because I'm still single, worse luck! But gosh we used to discuss sex enough before you married. Oh I'm sure Mark would make a most gentle and tender lover ....

And talking of Mark, here's the news I've been dying to tell from the start! He's being an absolute peach to me again. He was being very sweet indeed before we broke up for Christmas but then came a patch of disinterest – on his part only! Now, however, he's become friendly again. Last week I spent a lunch hour in Foyles and found a bargain Sibelius Symphony No 5 – remember it? – I couldn't really afford to buy it but then I couldn't afford not to buy it, so persuaded an assistant to take five bob deposit while I rushed back to borrow the rest from Dickie or one of the girls. Just my luck only Fanny Adams and Mark were in the office. I certainly wasn't going to ask F.A. any favours and when Mark wanted to know what all the panic was about and I told him, he insisted on giving me the whole amount and more, so I could buy the record and have some lunch as well. Wasn't that sweet of him, the darling.

Back I rush to the shop, buy the record, stuff myself with a couple of sandwiches and then back to the office fifteen minutes late! Mark knew what it was all about and didn't make a fuss but Fanny Adams caught me coming in and tore me off a strip. Back in the office found Mark sitting on the corner of my desk waiting to look at my buy. He agreed it was a bargain and took my breath away by suggesting I BROUGHT IT DOWN TO HIS PLACE so he could hear it!!

I laughed and said "with pleasure" not really thinking he was serious, but at the end of the day he asked if I'd be free to bring down the record at the weekend. I nearly had a fit! And I could have cried with frustration because we were having Uncle Manny and Auntie Rose down and I had to stay home. When I told him I couldn't come he said not to worry, perhaps I'd loan him the record sometime.

But yesterday – he took me to see a film of the Bolshoi Ballet dancing excerpts from various ballets. I've seen it twice already but didn't tell him that! Then we went to a rather nice restaurant nearby and had a meal; funny isn't it, I do so like my food but can't eat when I'm with him; nerves and excitement just makes my appetite disappear.

As I'd originally planned to meet Nadia for a bite and chat, had to phone and explain change of plans and she wasn't very pleased at being ditched and gave me a lecture about wasting time, being led up the garden path, getting involved with the wrong sort etc. She really hasn't anything to worry about because this friendship with Mark could never go very far, certainly not as far as I'd like! After all why should such a wonderful guy ever bother himself seriously over the likes of little me? But a girl can dream can't she ….?

Haven't heard a word from Maurice since Christmas but I'm not particularly heartbroken, whereas Mum and Dad are disappointed that nothing's coming from our friendship. I know they've discussed us with Sylvie and Ralph. I wonder how different Maurice would have been had his parents been alive to bring him up because Sylvie's obviously spoilt him. She's had to cope with him since he was ten, and although she gets on my wick sometimes I think she's been a real brick to devote herself to Maurice. If anything happened to our Mum and Dad, God Forbid, I couldn't see Connie dedicating herself to my well being! And Ralph deserved a medal too don't you agree? There aren't many men who'd take on his girlfriend's brother when they marry. Gosh it gives me the creeps to think there's so many people whose parents died when they were kids … Norma for one, Maurice and our Stan.

Hope the knitting patterns come in handy and the socks fit Dovoud although how a hot-blooded Persian can have cold feet I'll never know! Spoke to your Mum (to find out size of socks) and she sounded fine. She's asked Nad and me round for supper one day and we're looking forward to it.

Think I've told you all the news, must finish now, have some work to do for Fanny Adams and stencil for Dickie. Wouldn't think I was <u>Mark's</u> secretary would you, the way I'm made to do everyone else's work.

Love to Dovoud, keep well,
God bless, Lyn.

Dearest Norma,

I'm writing this in a state of terror after hearing the news tonight. The situation in the Middle East is growing worse every minute. This morning when we read the papers we were stunned. On the train to work and even at the office everyone had a long face; it isn't going to be easy for us to win we're so small and unequipped. The Arabs have been stocking up with weapons for ages and everyone's on their side. Just supposing they've got the Atom bomb hidden away somewhere! Have you ever read "Hiroshima" by John Hersey? I came across it in Foyles. Mummy caught me crying while I was reading it and asked why I was snivelling over a story. The trouble is, the story's fact not fiction.

Even Connie's solemn this evening; this turn of events has brought her down to earth with a bang. What with the excitement of her engagement party (yes, isn't it marvellous she's going to marry Stan!) and talk and daydreaming about the future, she hasn't given a thought to anything else. Now, all of a sudden she finds life very grim, just supposing all our boys go to help Israel as they're bound to do, Stan's just the type to pack his bags and go!

Sorry I've not got round to writing you the news about the engagement sooner, but work's been absolutely hectic with various trade shows and new campaign books to get out. Nothing exciting or special about the films but they will cause a lot of work.

About Connie, you'll be delighted to hear she's to become, all being well, Mrs Stanislav Padarowsky. Quite a mouthful after being plain Miss Connie Ash isn't it? Stan's parents came from Poland altho he was actually born in Whitechapel; I'm surprised he hasn't changed his name to something more English and easier to pronounce. Of course there's no chance of them getting married for ages but Connie's been blossoming from head to toe since he popped the question and you'd think there wasn't another man as wonderful as her Stan. Her devotion's shaken me I can tell you; in the past old Connie hasn't exactly been given to thinking of anyone else other than herself. Now she even rushes home to cook Mum and Dad a meal before they come in from the shop, and the way she manoeuvres the cleaner around the house you'd think she had been doing it since birth!

But let me tell you about the party, it was a swell affair in Kilburn. Connie looked like a Princess, no a Queen! She's so tall and slim, not a shrimp like me. And her hair had been swept upwards bouffant-like style which is all the rage, and she wore a royal blue dress. My dress was a sea-green chiffon and looked rather dreamy if I say so myself.

Nadia looked very glamorous in red, and was with her Isadore, and Phil was a peach and kept me company when I wasn't dancing with various uncles and boy cousins. I've always been fond of Phil and David, especially David. And not so long ago Nad was a right twerp and said Phil fancied me and if I played my cards right something might come of it and wouldn't it be marvellous we'd be sisters! Anyway there were endless "Please God by you!" thrown at me from all sides, tons of drink, nosh, and the band was noisy and good and everyone thoroughly enjoyed themselves. Dear Connie hasn't quite recovered yet and is still going around in a dream which is just the way I like it. She doesn't boss me half as much as she used to, and even offers to let me use her nail varnish and perfume!

How I wish a miracle would happen and Mark fell in love with me! Oh I know it'll never happen in a thousand years but dreaming's for free. On the other hand is anything impossible? You never thought you'd ever get to the States did you, yet there you are in Houston. As for Belle and Dovoud getting hitched, with all the obstacles in their way that really did seem an impossibility. And after all, I never ever dreamt Mark would take me out by myself and that <u>has</u> happened but how I wished he had been at the party with me. I thought of him all the time.

But for more startling news from the home front. Yesterday Sylvie came over in tears and told Mum (in the kitchen but I overheard) that she thinks she's fallen! She's absolutely furious because she's just beginning to have quiet nights with Jon. Apparently she and Ralph aren't talking at the moment. I heard her telling Mum how selfish men are and how she told Ralph at the time not to be so stupid but he said everything would be okay. Mummy would've had fifty fits if she'd known I was in hearing distance! But Sylvie and Ralph absolutely adore Jonathan and I know once she becomes used to the idea Sylv will be delighted about the new baby.

Mind you, I was rather disappointed in her recently. Mrs Hubbard of 25 has put her house up for sale and one of the viewers last week was a chap from Ceylon. When he offered a deposit to Mrs H, she told him it was already sold. She did this, Sylvie explained, 'cause there are enough foreigners in the neighbourhood already and the Close is the only place not "invaded". I was furious at this attitude and told Sylvie as much but she said I'm too young to understand and wait until I had property of my own! But can you imagine what the reaction would be if that person had been Jewish and Mrs Hubbard acted in the same way? All hell would be let loose!

Must go now and pack. I'm spending the weekend at Brighton, going up on the ten o'clock tomorrow. Bet I know what the main topic of conversation will be down there because Uncle's a shining light on the local Magen David Adom Committee. Poor Zaida's been ill with congestion of the lungs and Auntie Rachel's having a bad time with Judy which doesn't help any. She thinks I'll do some good if I come down and keep Judy company. Personally I'm on Judy's side, after all it can't be much fun for her having an ill old man in the house so she can't bring home friends or put on her radio after work. The burden of Zaida is making Auntie tired and she takes it out on Judy who answers back and then there's trouble but what can anyone do?

Judy wants to work in London and share a flat with a girl friend but Auntie and Uncle won't hear of it and until she's twenty one, which like me, isn't for ages, she hasn't a leg to stand on. Naturally they wouldn't dream of sending Zaida to an Old People's Home. Bless him, he can't help the way he is. Mum and Dad would have him if it were poss, but who'd look after him while they were at the shop?

Must just tell you I've read an article in a Sunday newspaper about English girls in the States. It seems that on the whole you're setting a good example. Carry on the good work chum! Cheerio for now, let's hope this war scare will be over by the time you receive this letter.

Keep ever so well and write soon, Lyn

Golden Realm Films.

Muzzeltov, muzzeltov, muzzeltov! A
thousand more good wishes to you both
dearest Belle,
     What absolutely marvellous,
terrific, stupendous news! Thank
goodness I read your note at home and
not on the way to work as I usually do.
At least I was able to dance around the
room with joy. When I shouted out the
news, Connie said, "Not wasting any
time is she!" Mummy said, "I hope
she'll be a sensible girl and take care
of herself", and Daddy asked, "What are
you snivelling about now?"
     Couldn't help it, (I'm shedding a
tear now!) of course I've thought about
the time you'd be a Mum, but now it's a
reality I feel all weepy. Just wait
until I tell Nad, I tried to get her
earlier but the line's engaged. I'll be
seeing her at the Film Café lunchtime
and she'll be thrilled with the news.
I'll go down to Mr Goodman in a minute
and tell him too.
     If there's anything you want i.e.
patterns of baby clothes, nappies,
talc, then let me know won't you? What
am I talking about, by the time you
want nappies you'll be over here. You
are going to have the baby here aren't
you? I wonder what, sorry who you want
most, boy or girl? And have you given
any thought to a name yet? Oh Belle,

don't you think it's incredible
yourself, that you're going to produce
a child????

I'm certainly going to have an
exciting time what with you and Sylv,
yes Sylvie across the road of all
people – expecting babies, and I'll
expect you to keep in even closer touch
than ever with me so I know how you're
keeping.

Oh bother, better sign off now,
Creeping Jesus is hovering around
outside and as he and Fanny had words
yesterday he's not in the best of
moods. I'll get this letter off to you
straight away (I'll give Billy two choc
biscuits to take this to Post now!)
because I want you to know of my
happiness. Of course I'll write again
very soon and until then, be careful!
Give Dovoud a big kiss for being such a
clever boy!

All my love,

Lyn.

Top of the morning to you dear Norma,
hope you're okay. I really ought not
write because it's your turn but I've
such smashing news I can't wait any
longer. Our Belle's expecting! Isn't it
terrific - sometime in December; she
and Dov can't agree on the exact date
but December's the month so perhaps
it'll be a Chanukah present! Phoned her
family to wish them Muzzeltov and Mrs
Hyam cried because she wants to see
Belle which isn't surprising.

 The sky's grown quite dark outside
and it's only four o'clock. I'm not
looking forward to the journey home,
the pelting rain, the packed tube, the
damp wait for the bus. Ah Barbie's just
come in with some tea slopping it all
over my desk on purpose I bet! I'll
tell you about her in a moment ...
Mark's in with Creeping Jesus
discussing this business of Dickie.

 Dickie's trouble started a couple
of months ago when a Norwegian chap
turned up in here wanting campaign
books on our most recent distr. He's
from a film mag and if I tell you he's
tall, tanned, blonde with gorgeous blue
eyes, flashing white teeth and hefty
shoulders, you'll know Dickie's
reaction to him! Before anyone had the
chance to ask the fellow what he wanted
Dickie was out of his chair like a shot

and had the chap's name and address in his diary and was promising to deliver the goods personally that very evening!

Sally and I nearly wet ourselves laughing and the thing is, Dickie just didn't make any secret of his intentions. Well to make a long story short this Norwegian and Dickie obviously hit it off because they've been "going steady" ever since and the chap comes to the office most nights to collect Dickie. Fanny Adams has decided that, brilliant writer or no, Dickie must go before he leads us girls astray. Mark however, just won't hear of him being fired and is in the Lion's Den this very second having words with Creeping Jesus on the subject.

As for Barbie! Although she's a bitch I think in the long run she's done me a good turn. Y'see for some time now she's been throwing hints that Mark has his eye on her – not that I'm surprised, she's got plenty for him and others to look at! But of course I preferred not to take her seriously. Then Sal and I were having a gossip and Barbie put her fat head around the door and we told her to clear out which made her furious and she said, "All right if you don't want to hear something interesting" – which we did, so we let her in.

The "something interesting" turned out to be that she'd been in the Stills Room with Mark when he'd suddenly lunged at her and kissed her and made arrangements to take her out that very evening. Can you imagine how I felt, pal? I didn't talk to Mark for the rest of the day and when it was home time left on the dot and spent the night crying like a fool. Next morning I still didn't speak to him except when it was absolutely nec, and eventually it must have sunk into his head that something was up because at last he asked what was the matter.

I don't know how I had the pluck really but I said that I thought it would be wise for him to ask Barbie not to spread around news of their "association" because it wouldn't do his prestige any good. Fancy me talking to him like that, I still can't get over it! I must admit he showed every sign of being genuinely amazed (probably at my cheek) and said he didn't know what on earth I was on about and would I like to start all over again! By this time I was trembling with fright so told him to forget it and had to rush to the loo - but I was so relieved at his reaction, reassuring myself that Barbie must have been making it all up, but then I came back from Contracts the same afternoon to find Barbie sitting on my desk swinging her gorgeous legs provocatively and looking extremely confident of her charm. Oh she makes me sick! But I told her in no uncertain terms where to go and she left post-haste. So I started to ignore Mark all over again and yet another night of tears!

The following day, except for dictation, neither Mark or myself had anything to say, but in the middle of the afternoon when he came out with some work for me Barbie came bursting into the office Mark suddenly exploded – at her! He told her that if she came in without first being summonsed, he'd see to it that she was transferred to another department. Barbie slammed the door behind her and Mark looked at me grimly.

"Well, does that satisfy you?" he demanded. I was struck dumb and could just about shake my head. What was I to conclude from his attitude Norma except that he actually cared what I thought about him? And my cup runneth over when, as I made to go home, he suggested I kept Good Friday free to spend with him! It was only when I was on the train going home thinking about it that all the joy drained from me … Norma, Good Friday was also first Seder night...

How did you spend Pesach? Did you go to Irvine for Seder Night, and do they make as much business of it in the States as over here? I wish I could emigrate before the hols while Mum's changing everything over. First she must spring-clean the entire house then there's the schlepping up and down of crockery, pots and pans and so on. Connie's been a real giggle, watching the process with keen eyes so that she knows exactly what's she's supposed to do when she gets married. What's worrying her most is the expense involved because Stan's wage isn't great and buying special Passover goods amounts to quite a sum. Personally I think it's crazy having to swap such things as sugar, etc etc., just because they must have a special label for the occasion. I mean to say, who'd be any the wiser if you didn't bother?

Daddy took Seder of course and Maurice, home for the holiday and being the youngest male present, said the Ma Nishtana. It was Stan's first time with us and Connie was enormously happy. Sylvie and Ralph were on good terms for a change and Jon billed and cooed for most of the evening. Auntie Carol, Shirl and Ivor were over but Shirley wasn't much fun because she wanted to be with Paul who was spending the evening at his Synagogue Chairman's house. At the end of the Seder when everyone kissed everybody else, and Stan and Connie making a meal of it, I felt all weepy because I wanted Mark. Fortunately Maurice is still enamoured with the girl he met at Christmas and was happy to give me a brotherly kiss and leave it at that.

I spent the second night at Nadia's and you can imagine what a riot that was! Not only was there a heap of Aunts and Uncles all over the joint but it seemed a dozen friends or more, yet Mrs S coped with the whole magillah as if entertaining en masse was an everyday event. The boys put three trestle tables together which stretched right through the dining room and lounge and as there was a shortage of chairs, David, Phil and a couple of Uncles had to sit in deckchairs, and I shared a Haggada with Phil and his current girlfriend Joanne. Did I ever tell you I saw David out with a blonde girl? Well she was there and her name's Greta. She's a real beauty, delicate features, lovely figure but oh, when she opens her mouth, a real cor blimey! Nadia says she doesn't fancy either girl as a sister in law and wanted to tell the boys as much but I pleaded with her to keep the peace. Peace in the Samuel household? Like asking for the moon!

All Yetta's kids were there even to the new baby who was an absolute peach and didn't make a sound all evening. Yetta let me hold him for a spell and he was so soft and warm. I'm longing for the time when I'll see Belle's baby.

Sleep was almost imposs that night. I was stuck in between Greta and Nadia and it was like a furnace. Sylvie was next to Nadia and kept complaining she was more out of the bed than in. Unable to sleep I thought of Mark (when don't I!), what would he have made of us if he'd been at the Seder table? He's never struck me as being a very spiritual type and I don't think he goes to church. I hope he doesn't!

It was a long time before anyone settled down; the boys in the next room - Isadore was staying the night - were telling each other stories (dread to think what kind!), and we could hear them killing themselves laughing. Incidentally, Greta was wearing a stunning black nightie; I don't know if she hoped to show it off to David if so she was out of luck poor girl! Mrs Samuel was an absolute gem because she got the boys to bring up tea in the morning. We had egg and chips for lunch and then tottered out for a stroll and then when we got home dear Mrs S. had put on a wonderful spread, smoked salmon, chopped herring, matzos of course. Wonder if Mark likes chopped herring or gefilte fish or if he's heard of them even? I was so pleased the Holidays came on a weekend so that I didn't have to miss work and be away from Mark, not seeing him on Saturday and Sundays is really frustrating.

Ah here he is returning from seeing the Chief and it seems he's got worked up for nothing because Dickie's outside in the general office collecting his stuff together having had an almighty row with Creeping Jesus. He's announced he isn't having his personal life discussed or arranged by the likes of them and has told them both a few home truths before resigning! Mark looks absolutely furious. Dickie's a good writer and gets on well with the Press boys; they know his peculiarities of course, some of them are the same! But it's never worried them. I shall miss Dickie because I confided in him how I felt about Mark and he's always been sympathetic. I wonder who'll come in his place. Oh I do hate changes.

Later.

Everyone's gone home but I'll just finish this letter so it can go off first thing tomorrow. Thought you might be interested to know I've palled up with Brian Levy again and he really is a nice person. We've had a sandwich and coffee together several times lately and he's asked me to go to a show with him one evening. There's several I want to see but I told him I'll think about it. Must be well over a year since I've been on a date with him.

Remember the afternoon when you and I had a date with him and his pal Cecil and when we asked where we were going he said home to meet his Buba? You roared with laughter and said: "Oh

well that's a change from being taken
home to see your etchings!" but the
laugh was on us because when we arrived
at his magnificent house, remember? His
dear little Buba <u>was there!</u>

And I can still remember what a
fool I felt when I asked if I could
help get tea and at that very moment in
came tea … wheeled on a trolley by a
real live maid in frilly white apron
and cap! That's the schmatte trade for
you. I really think Brian and I might
have grown closer had I given him half
the chance, but at the time I think I
liked David Samuel better and then, of
course, Mark came on the scene. Anyway
Brian seems far nicer now than even in
the old days, although I'm still not
madly interested.

Last time I visited Brighton I
told Auntie Rachel that I still hear
from you and they send their love. We
had good times down there together
didn't we? Everyone's fine except for
Zaida who grows more poorly every month
and Auntie says she wouldn't be
surprised if next winter doesn't finish
him off. Poor old thing, seems
incredible he's the same jolly man who
used to pinch my cheek and give me
spending money at the workshop when I
was a kid. We couldn't talk much
because his English was so limited and
I can't speak Yiddish, but he used to
take time off to walk me down the
street to Feuerstein's for sweets - and

his racing papers. I never could make out how he managed to read the racing news and make bets when he could neither read or write English, and yet he always had a winner!

Of course Auntie and Uncle raved about the Engagement Party and think Stan's a real mench and want to know when I'll find a nice boy for myself. When I said "all in good time" Auntie said if I didn't hurry up she'll do something about it. I told her if she tried any matchmaking it'd be a long time before they'd see me at Brighton again! Gosh, can you imagine Auntie and Uncle's reaction if they knew I loved Mark? They'd be every bit as heartbroken as Mum and Dad because I've been very close to them; closer than Connie who hasn't been down to stay half as much as me – she and Uncle don't hit it off, probably because they're both inclined to be bossy types.

It's really dark outside now and still raining. Wish Mark had stayed behind with me but I think he has a date. If he's with some girl then I hope she drops dead, oh no don't mean it! Someone fussing around outside the door, must be Fanny Adams waiting for me to go. Well she'll just have to wait. I think she'd charge me for using the typewriter after hours if she had her way. Please write soon,

God bless, Lyn

Hi there dear Norma,

So glad that someone is having a ball!
This Irvine sounds absolutely perfect
for you especially as he's one of us!
Who was he buying smoked salmon for,
and why were you serving? What do you
do - come home from the office and
slice the salmon and weigh a portion of
chopped liver? I remember in one of
your first letters after arriving in
Houston saying a definite no to helping
in the Deli!

You don't know what you are
missing over here, bedlam and chaos!
We're inundated with trade shows and a
Première or two - I'm talking about
British Lion and ourselves fighting
each other for venues and appropriate
dates.

Mark has been on the phone most of
the day and has had Creeping Jesus and
Fanny Adams on his back since he
arrived this morning.

As if that isn't enough to cope
with, there's a great scandal going the
rounds... dealings between renting and
distributing firms. Us included! Talk
of extra cash, luxury flats, hostesses
even - given in exchange for favours!
Apparently someone who's been sacked is
broigus and getting his or her own back

by spilling the beans and the papers are making a meal out of it! But I really can't believe we've done anything wrong.

On top of everything to contend with there's been a horrible experience with Mark. CJ knows all about the High Holy-days but I thought I ought to mention it to Mark. The very morning I decide to do so he brings the subject up himself but not in the way I'd have chosen. He dictated some correspondence including letters to two cinema managers one in Stamford Hill who was arranging an organ recital before the main picture show and the other in Stoke Newington who was having a local beauty contest. Having read back my shorthand so everything was clear I went to start work when Mark suggested, "Better do Krieger and Goldman's letters first so they can go off pretty sharply. They're Jews and will be taking time off soon, a fast or something". He was talking to me as if I was an ignoramus and then added, "I've had lunch with them, good managers, but they like their food, make a change for them to go without..."

I suppose it wasn't a terribly spiteful remark but what he said was unnecessary don't you think? Anyway it hurt me and I couldn't let him get away with it. I can't remember exactly what I said but something like, "Actually

they aren't the only ones going without
their food... there are hundreds of
Jews without food and it's got nothing
to do with a religious Fast either!"
and then I took a deep breath and told
him I would also be away soon, first
for Rosh Hashana and then Yom Kippur.

Oh Norma was his face a picture!
I've never seen him so put out but
instead of feeling glad I'd put him in
his place I wanted to cry. I longed to
rush to him and say not to worry but
instead rushed up to the loo. The fact
that I'm Jewish hasn't cropped up
before and why should it, it has no
bearing on the way I work or behave.
And it so happens that the holidays
have never caused any difficulties; in
the past Mark's been away himself on
holiday or the Festival has been at the
weekend. Do you remember how fed up we
were that a new man was coming to take
Mr Leslie's place and when Mark came we
were all prepared to give him the cold
shoulder.

Anyway, I eventually came back to
the office and Mark called me in and
asked me to excuse his bad manners! I
managed to accept his apology by
nodding my head. He didn't say anything
when I returned after the New Year but
when I came back after Yom Kippur he
actually looked pleased to see me.
"Glad you haven't faded away!" he
greeted smiling. What a smile! But a
little while later he called me in and

the smile was gone. Personnel had phoned down about my application for a transfer — yes Norm, I'd actually gone and done it! And he wanted to know why I was suddenly dissatisfied in Publicity. And then, wonderful, Mark suggested we had coffee after work to discuss the situation and of course I leapt at the invitation.

Once we were in the street together... TOGETHER isn't that a marvellous word? He said that if I could spare the time we might as well have a meal, so I phoned Mum from the restaurant and told her I'd be late because there was such a heap of work to catch up on after being away!

We went to a place just around the corner from the office. They must know Mark very well because the Head Waiter came running and the service was excellent. Mark was all charm and asked if I'd heard any good music lately and did I know there'd been open air concerts down by the Embankment? Did I know! Haven't I spent many an evening sitting in a deckchair listening to the music and thinking of him! Mum and Dad can't understand why I want to sit out in the cold listening to music when I can hear it in the comfort of home. Naturally Mark wanted to know why I'd asked to be moved. Was it, he wondered, because of his comment about Krieger and Goldman? I could hardly tell him, "It's because I love you chum and

you're driving me mashigah!" How could
I? So I said it was because I was fed
up working in an overcrowded and stuffy
office. There are three other
typewriters all clattering together and
whenever I want some fresh air and open
the window someone comes along and
closes it.

I should have kept my mouth shut
because next morning when I arrived it
was to find my desk and stuff had been
moved into Marks office! Whereupon he
told me I should now have a quieter
life and could have the windows open
whenever I want! Oh Norm, can you
imagine how I felt - a mixture of joy
and panic! I have only to look across
the room and there he is! How I long to
throw my arms around him... but no I'm
being very professional and only speak
when spoken to. But all this doesn't
make for concentration when concocting
my captions and items for the Campaign
magazine. Needless to say I've told him
I've withdrawn my request to move
elsewhere (for the moment anyway) and
the beast didn't say a word just nodded
rather smugly I thought as if he knew I
could never leave him!

Oh lor will have to go, work to be
done but before I finish I must just
tell you something about your charming
Promotions Manager. During the morning
when I was in the office, the phone
rang and it was one of his starlets
under contract and he chatted to her in

that smarmy way of his making arrangements to meet her after work to discuss "business". Oh yeh? He'd no sooner said goodbye than he phoned his wife and without as much as blinking an eyelid, told her he had to stay late for a meeting with Creeping Jesus. What a rotten liar! And his wife's such a sweet little soul. I've met her at a Première. Makes you wonder just how many other bosses give their wives the same story as Charlie gave his.

Waiting impatiently for a letter from Belle. Please don't let me wait too long to hear from you.

Love, Lyn.

Golden Realm Films
OR PARADISE!

Hello, hello, hello!

It's a grand day for singing, the sky
is blue above, the birds sing hello,
de-dum-de-dah, and everyone's falling
in Love, in Love, in LOVE! (with
acknowledgements to State Fair!) No I
haven't gone round the bend dear Belle,
except perhaps with happiness.

Sorry I haven't written sooner but
I've been in a sort of a daze. You see
I've been with Mark so much lately and
he's so sweet it's unbelievable! We're
working harder and closer together
because Mark's been doing Dickie's work
as well as his own – Dickie having left
us after a squabble with C.J. and we've
been staying late at the office to
finish things off. I don't mind
overtime one scrap 'cause he usually
takes me for coffee and sometimes a
meal before I eventually go home. I've
also met him at weekends to go to a
concert or film, and then last Monday I
actually went to a dance with him!

It was something to do with the
Film Publicity Club and terribly
exciting because it was at the
Piccadilly and I rubbed shoulders with
all the stars. Anna Neagle, Christine
Norden, John Gregson, Anthony Steele,

they were all there. Mind you, I only had two dances with Mark (just as well, I almost fainted when his arms came around me, aaaah!), the rest of the time I sat and listened to him talk shop with other film people.

Valerie Cripps was there and also danced with him but thank goodness she was with another party and didn't sit at our table. And after all, it was me Mark saw safely to the station to catch the last train and, oh darling Belle, he kissed me! K-i-s-s-e-d me right here on my cheek when he said goodnight. Talk about floating on air; I went home feeling as if I was sitting on a cloud rather than in a stuffy old tube train. Alas the excitement was too much for me and the following morning I was fit for nothing except bed. Mum decided to stay home most of the day and was around when Mark phoned to find out what was wrong. Later Mum wanted to know why he was so interested in my welfare (I'd told her I'd gone dancing with Brian Levy) and I retorted: "He is my boss after all!" Then she complained I am getting rings under my eyes from working so late at the office and she didn't see the need for it and, "Does your Mr Butler stay late too?"

My Mr Butler! I can tell you my stomach turned right over at the suspicion in Mum's voice. Was she, for some reason or other, beginning to think things? You can imagine how scared I was, Belle, because if she ever thought I cared for Mark, even a scrap, she'd make sure I left here. Anyway I tried to sound scornful and said Mark went home with the rest and thank goodness for that because I had quite enough of his bossing during the day without having to put up with it after hours! I laid it on as thick as I could and I think she was reassured, but to be on the safe side I decided that, for a few days anyway, I'd get home on time and keep away from Mark.

But yesterday evening I returned to the old and heavenly routine of staying late, and when work was finished we had a snack together and walked down to the Embankment and sat awhile in the park watching people walk by. We sat on a rather hard bench, nattering for a few minutes and then he suddenly put his arm around my shoulders! I could hardly see, hear or breathe from shock! And then he was actually inviting me to meet some friends of his this coming weekend. So do you blame me for being madly HAPPY, because although I've told myself again and again not to jump to conclusions, count my chickens, make mountains out of molehills and all the rest, I can't help thinking he <u>must</u> like me to want to introduce me to his friends...

Mind you, I'm terrified at the prospect and can't think what I should wear. Dress and jacket, my grey flannel suit? Wish I had a little black dress, I've nagged Mum often enough and she has the right material in the shop, but she says black's too old for me. At the mo Mum and Dad aren't on very good terms. Their shop assistant Eileen has been nicking material and Dad wants to send her packing. Mum wants to give her another chance because she has a couple of young kids; Mummy also worries in case Eileen goes around being nasty about our mob because a Jew's sacked her...never mind she's a gonif, and not for the first time either! Last year she helped herself to four yards of taffeta and had the cheek to pinch zip, binding and cotton to complete the outfit!

It's really quite sickening you know, this always having to mind our p's and q's because we're Jewish. There was a great prominence in an evening paper given to a Jewish couple who were caught cuddling on the back seat of their car a few weeks ago, but I noticed there were only half a dozen lines in small print about a couple who'd tied their toddlers arms and legs together to stop him from getting under their feet! And yesterday there was a small column about a Vicar who'd stolen Church funds for his own benefit. My golly, if that had been a Rabbi can you imagine the headlines he'd have made?

Mind you, everyone's being very sympathetic to the Israeli cause, our

Youth Clubs having a big dance at the end of the month and sending all the cash to the MDA, and Sally's Young Christmas Club is doing something similar, very decent of them.

Nearly forgot to tell you the most important thing of all! Nad and I went round to your Mum and Dad for a meal and had a lovely evening; your Auntie Millie came in for a little while and gave us the whole megillah about your cousin Sophie getting engaged to the best looking, cleverest, wealthiest Jewish boy in the whole British Isles! Afterwards your Mum told us Auntie Millie found him for Sophie by going to a Schiddach-maker. I just can't believe people still do that sort of thing in these days!

Need anything yet pal? Books about childbirth, motherhood etc.? I don't know how the book situation is in Persia; do they cost the same as here or more or are they as difficult to come by as sock patterns? Please don't hesitate to ask for anything you want. I hope the sickness has worn off – Sylvie's very sick and is complaining of a bad back. Ralph isn't much help to her, the big oaf. He's never lifted a finger to help in the past and doesn't mean to do so now. I hope Dovoud's taking care of you, I'm jolly pleased he's made you give up the job, you mustn't take any chances.

Had a very brief note from Norma and she's madly in love with a rather good-looking American called Irvine (she's sent a snap of them together) with whose family she spent Pesach, and between you and me I think it's all very serious. He's something in stocks and shares which can't be bad and has enough money to talk about taking our Norma to Canada for a holiday! I'd be happy if Mark took me to Brighton!

Signing off now Belle because I've tons of work to do and a trade show at three. I'll write again very soon and you do likewise, love to Dovoud,

God bless,
Lyn

How could you! What a letter to send me. You're being as bad as Nadia and I thought I could at least count on your understanding.

I can't help the way I feel about Mark and even if I weren't going out with him as you suggest, I'd still go on caring about him. All right so I "loved" Tony in Contracts when I first came to Golden Realm, and Bernie Susskind, and Nadia's David and loads of others – which teenager doesn't have crushes tell me? But honestly Belle, this feeling I have for Mark isn't soppy or shallow. Anyway what right have you to talk; look at the way you used to go goofy whenever Jeremy Segal came into the building, or Philip Sless, and what about Leon??? Oh you can't deny it, there were plenty of chaps you went dreamy over before Dovoud came on the scene. Tell me, how did you finally know Dovoud was the right one?

So you think it would be wiser for me to go with Brian or Maurice. Not on your life! First of all it would be completely unfair to let anyone get involved with me when I can only think of Mark, and secondly Maurice doesn't appeal to me at all. Please, please dear Belle don't lecture me again. I know you've my welfare at heart and thanks a million, but the only way you can help is by wishing me luck in the future and by putting up with my outpourings on paper – cheerful or otherwise.

At the moment I'm gloriously cheerful because Mark and I are so close! The friends he took me to see are really ducky. They live in Reigate and Gary is with M.G.M., he's been Mark's buddy for years and Gary's wife Brenda has also been in the film biz before they married. They've an absolutely terrific house with such an enormous garden you could get our house and garden into the grounds a dozen times over and still have space to spare, no kidding. They've a cook, daily and a gardener. It seemed as if we spent all afternoon walking around the flowerbeds and through the rose garden and orchard, but I enjoyed it because the weather was fine and Brenda was nice to me as soon as I arrived. Incidentally I wore my grey suit and a pink short sleeved sweater, bought some new lipstick and varnish to match, and I think I looked okay.

Brenda must be in her late twenties and great fun and she had lots to tell me about Mark, how he and Gary had been friends since after the war when they met in their first job in a Press agency, how they'd holidayed together abroad and how they still saw a lot of each other, lunches etc. It did dawn on me then that I'd spoken to Gary on the phone quite a number of times but not been particularly interested in his association with Mark; now if it had been a woman, I'd have remembered all right!

Brenda wanted to know all about little me and I felt terribly dull describing my routine, but it appears she'd never been more than a shorthand typist before marrying Gary and now she just potters around the "old homestead". They met at a Boating Exhibition (both are mad keen on sailing. Brenda's dad's ex-Navy) where Gary bought a very expensive looking motor boat!

Gary piped up, "I don't know to this day Marilyn, whether she fell in love with me or my boat!"

We had cold turkey supper with chilled wine in long glasses, the radio played softly, Mark sat opposite me looking absolutely adorable and all was heavenly. And then Brenda took me upstairs to powder my nose and told me how pleased she was I'd come because Mark had only once before brought a woman friend (???) to meet them. If I were at all interested, and she thought I was, this was a good sign! I went absolutely daft and told her just how I felt about Mark and she said I obviously had my head screwed on the right way because Mark was "a honey"! Of course, after spilling the beans, I wondered if I'd been wise, she would probably tell Gary and he'd tell Mark and that might well frighten him away altogether. Still it was too late to do anything about it, me and my big mouth!

We left at ten because of the journey home and Mark promised to bring me back another time. I don't have to tell you I wished and wished the wine had softened Mark into falling in love with me, but nothing happened. He drove me to the station as usual, saw me on to the train and that was that. But yesterday when he took me out Belle, oh that was different! A Sunday I'll never forget as long as I live.

I met him at Richmond and we went for a long ride into the country where we finally stopped for a picnic lunch packed by his illustrious "daily". I won't go into the small details but after the food we sprawled out on the grass for a snooze but neither of us closed our eyes. I don't know who made the first move, me I suppose! But the fact remains…we kissed! Oh Belle, do you remember the first time you and Dovoud kissed? Was it all you thought it would be? It was over very quickly, just a peck really, yet I felt as if I was drowning, but you can't drown for long in a field of bushes, buttercups and daisies and smelly cow dung!

The second time around I went quite daft and told him how much I "liked" him and prayed he'd tell me he loved me, but no fear! He just grinned and said he was glad I "liked" him because he'd been thinking rather a lot about me lately, in fact too much for comfort. I was deliriously happy! And then just as we were going to kiss again a rotten crowd of rotten kids came skipping past letting out rotten vulgar wolf whistles! When it clouded over we packed up and went back to Richmond and the Bungalow was just as I'd imagined, very small mind you, but cosy and bright. His daily, a Mrs Hunter, was still pottering around (she comes weekends too because she's a widow) and doesn't seem a bad old stick, and her son's rather luscious (he was messing around in the garden) and I think I went down well with him. But after tea they left and Mark and I were alone.

We didn't do anything much – worse luck! I mooched around behind him in the garden for a while until I felt too cold, then I sat and read the papers and was perfectly happy – until he said it was time for "high tea" and would show me where everything was! I nearly had kittens wondering what he expected me to do. What have I ever cooked but egg and chips? But I didn't let the side down Belle, and served up cold ham (!) baked beans and chips cooked to perfection! Then after we'd washed up together, we went into the lounge. An attractive lounge, cream walls, red carpet, shelves loaded with books, a three piece suite, red stuff very comfy. Are you thinking – ah ha, now what? I certainly did and was so excited I could hardly breathe, but I needn't have got so worked up, the obnoxious darling switched on the radio, shared out the Sunday papers and that was that! Don't men have any idea how we feel when we love them so much?

So you see pal, it's no earthly good you going on at me. Now that things are so promising between Mark and myself surely you can't expect me to call a halt?

I know what I wanted to ask you. Are you anywhere near that town with the tremors? It must be horrifying to be involved in an earthquake. I don't think England's ever had anything really serious; can't remember reading about earthquakes at school. I must ask Maurice sometime, he's very knowledgeable – and doesn't he know it! But he's a good boy at heart. Sylvie's told me he's keen on chucking his studying and going to Israel to help, if not with the actual fighting then on a Kibbutz. Wish I had the pluck to go and do my bit – cooking for the soldiers??? I certainly wouldn't be much cop doing first aid! But anyway I couldn't leave Mum and Dad for so long or my darling Mark. As for Stan, he'd be off like a shot if it wasn't for my big sister. Are the Persians pro-Israel or for Egypt? Egypt I reckon 'cause they're part of the Arab family aren't they?

Thinking of you and your precious cargo, write to me soon with your news, and no more scolding please!

Your pal,
Lyn.

Beautiful Belle and her Persian groom, married under a Tullis, in Douvoud's grandfather's garden.

Les Girls of Golden Realm Films

Tehran. Belles' new home and way of life.

Houston. Norma's brave move to the U.S.A

Petula Clark

H.R.H Princess Margaret meets
exotic screen star Jane Russell.

Anna Neagle and Michael Wilding

Van Johnsson 'our heart throb'

Mark keeping an eye on film star Joseph Cotton, taking a break during a personal appearance at at a West End cinema.

Passover Seder Night, a time of family gatherings around the world including London's east end.

Dearest Norma,

Thanks for your lovely long letter; I let Mummy read it
and she was very interested to know all about your life in
the States – quickly telling me not to get any ideas about
joining you! Well I might have thought about it once but
certainly not now Mark's being such a sweetie to me. But
I'll tell you about that later.

There's Belle first. You'd think she'd be satisfied
to take things easy in her state of health, wouldn't you?
But oh no, she's fed up with being a lady of leisure and
insists that she should be allowed to get on with
everything just like every other wife. Needs her brains
tested if you ask me. Did I ever tell you how excited she
was when Dovoud bought her a cooker of her very own?
You see when she married and took over the upstairs
rooms of her In-Law's house, it was taken for granted
that she and Dovoud would go down to Mama for meals
(this is the procedure in Persia, young couples have no
private lives of their own!) but instead of being happy
with this arrangement (I wouldn't object to someone
waiting on me!) Belle insisted she cooked Dovoud's food
herself. In fact she made such a commotion about it that
in the end Dovoud bought her a cooker and, honestly, she
raves so much about it at the time you'd have thought
he'd bought her a diamond tiara! What is good tho is that
she's learning Farsi. I think that is what it's called, and
eventually she'll be able to talk to everyone!

Dad's just poked his head around the door to say
my radio is on too loud, it's time to go to sleep and he's
fed up with finding all the lights on upstairs and when the
next electricity bill arrives he's going to give it to Con

and me to settle up! I've told him I'm writing to you and he sends his best wishes but I still mustn't be long!

I simply must tell you about Mark. We aren't only working hard together – I did tell you Dickie left G.R. and Mark's doing his work as well as his own? – but we seem to be <u>going</u> together! Oh no, he hasn't said anything in the remotest bit binding or conclusive about our friendship, no "I love you etc." worse luck, but we do spend most weekends together and several evenings, even if it's only for a couple of hours before eventually going our own way, and I've been to his home and he's kissed me. You aren't seeing things pal he's <u>kissed</u> me! Once some time ago and again more recently, and this time more profoundly, oh much more profoundly!

It was last Sunday to be exact. A heavenly day, weather wise and Mark wise! He met me in Regents Park (I'd told Mummy I was meeting Nadia and some friends, hate the deceit but what can I do?) and we just wandered around the park and London as if we'd never been there before. Well have you ever seen more than a passing glimpse of our Buckingham Palace or St. Paul's Cathedral? The interior is marvellous – Dad would have a fit if he'd known I'd been inside a church! Have you sat in a deckchair in Hyde Park or been in a boat on the Serpentine? Funny isn't it, tourists fall in love with our City while we go traipsing off abroad to visit monuments and museums, the like of which are on our very doorstep but which we don't see or appreciate. A case of familiarity breeding contempt I suppose.

It was a most glorious day and after a meal we went and collected the car and Mark said he'd drive me some of the way home because trains were bound to be full this summers night. I didn't dare hope he'd "pull over" somewhere along the way but he did! And to my delight, a delight which made my heart burst, he took me in his arms and kissed me properly – so properly I could barely catch my breath. No wonder Maurice and all the others have never moved me, I've never loved them!

But I came down to earth with a bang when he said he might as well take me all the way home and deliver me to the door. I got in a panic and confessed Mum and Dad didn't know I was with him and would be annoyed if they knew. Annoyed? That's putting it mildly! I guess Mark was rather huffy about this and wanted to know what all the hush-hush business was about. We've not mentioned religion in any depth 'cause it hasn't come up although it's been at the back of my mind many times. So I told him how we don't approve of serious friendships with anyone non-Jewish. I was so agitated that I don't think I explained it very well and instead of being understanding Mark said rather sharply, he hadn't thought such narrow-minded attitudes existed in this day and age. I suppose it's hard for an outsider to understand how our older generation feel on the subject. Like your own folk Norma (God rest their souls) my Mum and Dad come from Orthodox homes; when kids attended Shul every Friday night and Saturday morning; classes on Sunday, no writing or riding once Shabbas was in – the lot in fact! Our upbringing Con's and mine, hasn't been half as strict thank goodness, couldn't have borne it, but until we left school and went to work neither one of us were allowed to write once the candles were lit on Friday, and no going out either. Not being able to write was frustrating, but it was even worse that I couldn't switch on the radio and listen to music. Con used to go in the lav and do her nails!

So this evening ended with Mark taking me a fair distance before seeing me on to a train and the evening finished rather flat. But I'm going out with him tomorrow and hope we'll get back on dreamy terms. I'm disappointed that, seeing we're so close these days, he still chooses to see Valerie Cripps now and again. I try hard not to show my green eyes by asking where they've been together but deep down oh I boil! Now I know how Belle felt when she thought something might be going on between Dovoud and his old flame Mahi. Fortunately that problem died a natural death. My main worry is that V.C. is going away on holiday in two weeks time – the same time as Mark – and I really couldn't bear it if they're going to spend it together. I've not made any arrangements to go away this year and can't even get excited at the thought of a holiday because it means being parted from Mark. Sometime ago Connie came up with the crazy idea of hitch hiking from Paris to South of France. Well she can count me out, it sound too much like hard work, besides it means leaving Mark. Mind you now she's got Stan she's forgotten all about going abroad – unless it's on a honeymoon! Did I tell you she gave most of her engagement cheques to the M.D.A? (I bought her and Stan some linen). Nadia, crazy as usual, spent a couple of weeks helping on a Farm. She said it was fabulous, very earthy and bawdy and the crowd were great fun.

Yes, Dad, I've nearly finished! Looks as if I'll have to call it a day but not before I beg you to tell me how serious you are with Irvine. The only disadvantage I can see about you and him getting hitched, is that it means you'll never set foot on this land again unless Irvine brings you here for a honeymoon. Tell me what the weather's like, what you've bought lately, what music you've heard and does Irvine share your tastes?

Love from your inquisitive but loving pal,

Lyn

Valley View.

How's things with you Belle?

I'm fed up to the teeth! I didn't want to come down here
in the first place, Mark had asked me out for the weekend
but Con and Stan wanted to come for "old times sake"
and Mum insisted I came too with some idea of me being
chaperone. Have you ever heard anything so ridiculous -
gosh, if they wanted to misbehave how does she think I
could stop 'em? Mind you I'm sure Stan is far too
honourable to do anything improper with my sister, not
that I'd blame him for a mo if he tried his luck, it must be
a terrible strain to have to wait two whole years or more
to get married – all according to how long it takes them
to get some money together for a home.
        The crowd here are a load of twerps, all spotty,
playing at being big boys. One's taken a fancy to me,
Solly Goldstein, and he's being a right bore following me
around with gooey eyes. Connie's all cross with me for
being awkward but damned if I'm going to put myself
out for her still more!
        Darling Mark! How I wish he were here.....we
went down to Hamble not so long ago. His friends
Brenda and Gary moor their boat there and altho I know
nothing about boats I could see this one was a smasher. I
had no idea they could be so well furnished. Two double
bunks (which gave me lovely ideas!) a dining room suite
even a shower. The plan was for Gary to take us for a run
but, just my luck, the weather turned foul and after going
in circles (my stomach taking frequent steep dives!) we
returned to port and spent the remainder of the day in the
Yacht Club. Mark appeared to be enjoying himself but
then he knew various bods and likes a drink or two, just a

few mind you, but I must admit I was bored. Even Brenda was occupied with someone else and I just sat listening like a muggins. Felt terribly nondescript and disinteresting. The only thing which brightened the horizon was the thought of later….it having been arranged that we spent the night at Gary's, but oh, I might just as well have been in my own bedroom at home for all that happened!

I was put in the spare bedroom next to Mark's, Brenda and Gary were on the other side of the landing and naughty of me perhaps, but actually prayed he'd come to kiss me goodnight – and stay! I suppose I have to count myself lucky he gave my hand a squeeze and wished me goodnight. I didn't sleep a wink in case he came but I was asking for the moon, and then in the morning I got up before everyone else, washed all over and combed my hair and stuck on some lipstick just in case he might get a glimpse of me in bed. But the first we saw of each other was at the breakfast table and then he spent most of the time talking to Gary about boats and films.

Brenda, the dear, must have realized how I was feeling because she winked at me and whispered over the marmalade: "Everything comes to those who wait!" We had lunch with them and then Mark took me to his home where Mrs Hunter was expecting us for tea. Although her son's rather nice I don't like Mrs H. very much now. Everytime I come to the house she makes sure I remember she's in charge and during bits of conversation she lets drop how many other women she's entertained on Mark's behalf which, naturally, makes me boil with jealousy.

After tea she and her son went off, my having offered to wash up which I did while Mark pottered around the garden. When he came in he was all hot and damp from digging and smelt lovely. I absolutely ached to put my arms around him and then he came over and, wait for it, kissed me soundly on the mouth. Ah, I can feel him now!

"You look just right here, Miss Ash," he says grinning. "I've half a mind to offer you a permanent job in my kitchen."

"What's stopping you then?" I laughed back. "At least ask and let me have the chance to turn you down!"

Whereupon he shrugged and went to get himself cleaned up. Oh Belle, perhaps if I hadn't been so awfully awfully jolly, and only because I was scared and shy, he might have proposed!

But I really couldn't grumble about the evening because we listened to some records, danced a little with the light out and I nearly died of fright when he stroked the back of my neck. And to think I wanted him to seduce me! I guess I'm all talk because I don't know that I'd have the pluck, love him as I might, to actually go to bed with him .....

The point is nothing did happen except for him asking me to go to Tunbridge Wells with him one weekend! His father and sister live there.

Sally knows how I feel about Mark and is horrified. She came into the office the evening he left early to prepare for his holiday. She took one look at my face and rolled her eyes in despair and she, like you dear Belle, now often reads me the riot act not because of him not being Jewish, Sally isn't Jewish so she doesn't care about that, but because Mark is quite a bit older - but I don't care!

So you know what Connie and Stan are talking about? They're sprawled out here beside me nattering about honeymoons! Listen to this ... they'd like to go on a cruise to the West Indies, Greece and Israel. Who wouldn't but I'd like know what they intend to use for gelt. Daddy won't have anymore for them after spending a packet on the party and giving big donations to the M.D.A., and he's forever dishing out remnants and rolls of good material for Tombolas and Bazaars. That's the trouble with having a business, people expect you to give even if you're finding it hard to make ends meet and you've a family to feed. He and Mum haven't had a break and I'm sure the shop wouldn't collapse if they went away for a week or two. I offered to help Eileen take care of the joint but couldn't convince Dad I'll be able to cope. Oh yes, Connie would manage all right but not scatty little me!

Oh hell it's really sickening having to stay here seeing all the others having such a good time. Connie did try to make me bring Brian Levy along but I don't think he's a Valley View type, besides which it would mean getting involved with him and I don't want to do that. We have such a nice easy relationship at the moment, coffee and sandwich at times, an evening out now and again (when Mark's otherwise engaged), a goodnight kiss. Do you know something, I don't mind him kissing me, he doesn't take liberties. When Maurice used to get hold of me it was as if he wanted to eat me up!

Can't wait for you and Dovoud to come over; have you made any plans yet? I know your Mum's having your bedroom redecorated, and I bet the family will arrange a swell homecoming party. For goodness sake keep well and don't let me hear any more rubbish about being bored at home and depressed because you're looking such a mess. I'm sure you're as bonny and as beautiful as always. Think I've told you all the news and in any case the ribbon isn't much cop, mustn't complain we're lucky to have this machine here to use.

Connie and Stan send their love,

Lyn.

Dearest Norma,

Bonjour mon ami and all that jazz!
Would you believe it we did our
hitchhiking holiday after all. Mum
came up trumps and gave us some cash
and Fay worked on her family so off we
went. Mind you Mark was not amused at
having such short notice that I was
taking time off and I wasn't too happy
at having to leave him behind! And how
Connie could leave Stan I just don't
know!

I'm not bothering to tell you how
we got to France, suffice to say it
was stormy and hectic and a relief to
get back onto dry land. Fortunately
Connie had decided not to buy a return
ferry ticket in case we couldn't get
to the port in time.

Fay and I were all for finding a
room for the night but Connie wanted
to get walking. A couple of hours
later she came round to our way of
thinking and we took a room in a B&B,
shared a bed, had no sleep and back on
the road at dawn! I reckon it was
about three hours before we had our
first lift. A car with four chaps drew
up at our side and although they
couldn't speak a word of English (at
least that was the way they played it)

and we only knew a smattering of their lingo, we managed to make them understand what we wanted — the south of France!

We were getting on very nicely thank you when the chaps in the back with Connie and Fay started to get fresh. "Up my shorts without any preamble!" screams Fay, so big Sis slapped them away. I was o.k. in the front but I wanted to tell Connie not to lose her temper in case they got nasty (rape!) but as a matter of fact the boys just roared with laughter. Next thing we know the car stops and the boys suggest we all go for a swim. I can't tell you the name of the place but lots of greenery and a river. We told them with hand gestures we had no costumes and they indicated that didn't matter! When we continued with the emphatic non, non! they opened the car doors and told us to scram … we wouldn't have minded quite so much if they had put us down on a busy high road but there was just the countryside on one side of us and water on the other.

We must have walked miles before seeing another vehicle and that didn't stop and we had no idea where we were and I said we should have bought a map and that put Connie in a filthy mood. Fay and I did our best to keep a stiff upper lip by singing everything from "Yiddisha Momma" to Gilbert and

Sullivan but it wasn't long before our
repertoires, as well as our bodies
were exhausted. So we started on I-spy
but the whole trouble was there wasn't
anything to spy except trees, fields,
water and sky. I'm afraid even Fay's
good humour went to pot and there we
were tottering along in the heat,
silent and scowling and hungry! Is
this what you call a happy holiday?

Thank goodness our luck turned
and a kind lorry driver took pity on
us. A pleasant man but a ghastly
driver, so fast and spending his time
looking at us instead of the road! But
hooray, quite a long time later we
arrived in St Maxime all in one piece
but starving and weary. I suggested we
find some food and somewhere to stay
but Con, as usual had other ideas,
food yes but then the beach. So we
bought lovely French bread and pate
and bottled water and guzzled it on
the most gorgeous soft golden beach.
Needless to say we were so tired the
three of us fell asleep and when we
woke up we were so hot! I wanted to go
in for a swim and cool down but Fay
said we should find somewhere to stay
which of course was sensible. But it
wasn't easy, everywhere was full and
so expensive after all this was south
of France and St Maxime enormously
popular. But at last we found a couple
of beds in a joint resembling the
Black Hole of Calcutta! Connie's fault

because she held the gelt and went after the cheapest place there. Two beds, basin and a hole which was supposed to be a window. I won't tell you what the loo was like and no bath or shower. Fay, being on the bonny side had a bed to herself while Connie and I shared the other one.

Sorry pal have to do some work, write more later...

Hi there, do you want me to carry on? Well let me tell you dear Norma, we were almost goners! We had got sunstroke during those hours asleep on the beach. Fay was the worst because her bikini barely covered her private parts so you can imagine how much of her there was to burn. Connie and I were not much better I could hardly open my eyes and I really thought my head was going to explode and Fay's knees were like melons. I don't mind telling you there were times when I was scared, people have died from sunstroke and Fay was in a terrible mess. Thank goodness Mum had made us bring Calamine lotion with us so we absolutely smothered each other from head to foot. Connie wanted to call the doc but Fay said no fear in case it cost too much. Presumptuous of me to think my prayers helped us get better (I said the Shema) but did I pray and we pulled through "Thank

God"! How I longed for Mark. Was he missing me?

As soon as we could get back on our feet (and they were also sore!) we shoved our clothes in our bags - although they were soaking wet because we put them under the tap and over us to cool us down - and moved to a better hotel which was very comfy. I think the cost of the room might well have broken Connie's heart if she hadn't discovered there were four fellas on the floor above us, Jewish ones! And the staff were kind and gave us food in the room but Connie really wanted to go into the dining room to see if we could make contact. I said surely she couldn't be interested when she had left Stan at home. She didn't answer but if looks could kill! Of course we were worried about going out into the sun again but on the other hand who wanted to come all this way and end up in a hotel lounge?

To cut this long story short the boys upstairs turned out to be very pleasant, for a start they hired the umbrellas and sun loungers on the beach and made sure we didn't overdo the sun. They were all from Edgware and our ages. Three worked in the West End and by the time we had to make a move for home we had exchanged addresses and phone numbers. I said to Connie what was the point when she had a fiancé. "But YOU haven't anyone yet.

This might do you good", she said. I
didn't complain, there was no way I
could mention Mark. Better that I let
her get on with it.

Except for the thought of not
seeing Mark I would love to have
stayed longer. St Maxime is a really
great place, heavenly beaches, long,
wide and soft, a warm sea. White
buildings, dazzling in the sun,
yachts, plenty of money around – in
other people's pockets that is! It's a
shame we didn't think about coming
here together, you and Belle, Nadia
and me, what a super time we would
have had!

Starting back on our hitch home
was a giggle because the boys thought
it would be a lark to walk along with
us for a mile or two but they didn't
have enough stamina to keep up and the
drips soon turned back.

We had quite a walk before
getting our first ride and although
the lift took us some distance, Connie
didn't think we'd gone far enough for
one day and made us hike on. By the
time she was satisfied it was almost
dark and it took us ages before we
found a place for the night by which
time Fay and I were dead beat.
Furthermore Connie discovered she'd
come on and as this was a week early,
she was completely unprepared. Of
course all the chemists were closed
and she might have been in shtook if

I'd not had one of my brilliant ideas and sacrificed the padding in my sun dress bra!

We couldn't start out in the morning til chemists opened and it was ages afterwards before we got a ride by which time poor Connie was doubled up with pain. I suppose it was the walking combined with the sunstroke episode which was causing the trouble because normally she doesn't have any bother.

Incidentally I'm doing all this after work, everyone has gone including Mark having first reminded me about covering the typewriter when I'm finished. I just don't know why he is so concerned about this typewriter?

Anyway when we reached Lyons it was my turn to have a raging headache and the only room we could get was on the sixth floor sans lift … the room wasn't even big enough to swing a cat round in and as we had to share a bed you can imagine how hot and stuffy it was. By dawn I couldn't stand it any longer and got up to go for a walk. Connie continued to snore but Fay woke and insisted on coming along so there we were trotting around the block until we came across a Café which was just opening its shutters. The owner must have seen my green face because she ushered me in like a long lost daughter, gave me an enormous pill to take with a glass of water and

presumably told me to drink up. Some
job I can tell you because every time
I tried to swallow the pill old Fay
thumped me on the back and whispered
to spit it out. The crazy mixed up kid
thought they were trying to drug me
and ship me off for white slave
traffic!

Despite Fay, I swallowed the
tablet at last and the owner turned up
with heavenly black coffee for both of
us — and some French bread. That put
Fay in a panic because we only had a
few francs between us. But the woman
asked for nothing, gave us both a kiss
and a card with the name of her Café
if we were ever passing again!

Now if only there were more such
friendly and generous people in the
world what a marvellous place it would
be. Any French town at dawn is
fascinating and Lyons was no
exception. On the way back to the
hotel we saw water carts showering the
kerbs and when Fay smelt a bakery it
was all I could do to drag her away.
She is such a nosh pot. I don't know
where she puts it all.

Connie was wide awake when we got
back and she was livid with us for
going out without telling her first.
Supposing we hadn't come back, she
screamed, how would she know where to
look for us? She calmed down over a
gorgeous breakfast and more coffee
which did me good.

Con decided that if by noon we didn't seem to be making much progress on the road we'd have to use public transport. It was essential to reach Paris that night and be able to catch an early train the following morning. Luck was on our side for a change because we managed to hitch a fantastic ride to the very outskirts of Paris and were so bucked that we didn't even mind the prospect of walking across the city … mind you halfway we gave up and took some public transport. The driver who gave us a lift was in the French forces, an officer or captain, extremely smart and very well behaved!

Although I was absolutely dead beat, I couldn't think of an early night because heaven alone knows when I'd see Paris again, so we lashed out on a bath – all girls together hilarious – put on the freshest of our clothes and spent the entire night exploring the fabulous streets of Paris. We could have been picked up a dozen times as we went from one part of town to the other, walking and via Metro, but we clung together … dived into bistros for coffees, persuaded Con to slum and eat chips walking along and really had a bon, bon nuit! What commotion and fascination, you and Belle would have loved it! Midnight and all the shops still ablaze with light and colour, everyone laughing and walking and friendly, full of energy despite the hour (except for us!). Why on earth can't our West End be the same? Tourists to London must think our capital a dead loss. Between you and me I enjoyed that one evening more than the whole holiday put together, how I'd love to be there with Mark ... I missed him SO much!

Where would you go for a holiday in the States? Is Florida close by? I expect New York has wonderful stores and art galleries. How far is Hollywood? I've probably asked you this before! Well you've now heard all about my adventures so your next letter must be full of information about your life as it is now.

Of course Mum and Dad welcomed us back with lots of hugs and kisses, salt beef, latkes and cucumbers! But there was no kiss or hug when I arrived at work, Mark just gave me time to get my pad and pencil and then it was back to the grind. But as far as I was concerned nothing had changed, my heart thumping away as soon as I saw him.

I really must go home now so take care of yourself, love to your family and say "hello" to Irvine for me. Let me know what's going on in that area.

Love Lyn.

Dearest Norma,

What do you think of my holiday? Took
me some time to recover but I'm happy
to say Mark suddenly decided on a meal
out when he told me I'd been missed!
Hooray!
     But sad news about Shirley, her
American has returned to the States.
I've given him your address, but he
says it's a fair way from Georgia to
Houston. We all loathed to see him go.
You should have seen us at his last
service - we were all in tears, and it
wasn't only us, Shirley's family, who
were upset, but the complete
Congregation were moved at his
farewell sermon. On the evening before
his departure the Council gave a big
party in the hall (Shirl couldn't get
us invites but told us about it – in
tears) and, after saying how he would
miss everyone, added that he'd
definitely return because unlike
previous ministers, he had a very good
reason for doing so … and put his arms
around our Shirley and everyone
clapped!
     A few Young Marrieds took time
off from their various businesses to
drive to Heathrow with Shirley and

we've since heard it was awful saying
the final goodbye and even Paul's eyes
were wet. I've seen Shirley a couple
of times since and she doesn't seem
the same girl, all wan and lifeless.
That's love for you!

Nadia? Well there's nothing very
exciting happening to her. She's still
going out with Isadore and trying to
get me interested in one of his
cronies. And Belle? Her last letter
wasn't very cheerful, she's naturally
blossoming out and says she feels a
frump and is worried in case Dovoud
finds her ugly and starts to stray.
She says her In-Laws are wonderful and
no girl could have married into a
happier or more loving family, and
consequently she's terribly anxious
that they shouldn't be too hurt
because she wants to come over here to
have the baby.

Mrs Hyams is having Belle's
bedroom done up for when they come. I
wonder how Belle will enjoy living in
Commercial Road again after a street
in Tehran? I love it when I stay with
Nadia, it's so colourful and
interesting in the East End and so
dull at home. Nad says I need my
brains tested and if I lived in her
district all the time I wouldn't be so
enchanted.

Went to Valley View some time
back to "chaperone" Connie and Stan
and it was very dull and boring and I

could only think of Mark perhaps going out with Valerie Cripps because I'd had to turn his invite down. I did manage to write a letter to our Belle but forgot to tell her about your proposed trip to Canada with Irvine. Is it still on? And isn't it miles and miles away from the States? Do let me know all about it and don't forget to take snaps. And if you visit any waterfalls on the way (is it Niagara?) don't do anything crazy and stand on the edge!

I went to the flicks with Brian Levy recently and asked him why he isn't in his father's business. Apparently he doesn't get on too well with an elder brother who works with his Dad, and thought it better for everyone if he went into something completely different. Brian really is a very nice person and despite his money he has humility and that's a virtue wanting in quite a number of boys. He's not particularly happy at work not getting ahead fast enough and looking around for another job, but he wants to keep in films and especially down Wardour Street which, like the East End, has an atmosphere all its very own. Do you miss it by any chance?

Incidentally, Personnel have had their rooms redecorated and most of the toilets in the building are being cleaned up. We could certainly do with new taps and seats in our loo. Contracts now have the fourth floor to themselves and you wouldn't know Tony who has a big office of his own and is called "Sir" by all the youngsters! What's worrying me is the rumour that our department's to be renovated with a new office for Mark and an annexe for little me. Oh I don't want to be separated! Heaven alone knows why this work's going on because I read in the trade papers that the film business isn't doing all that well – and especially our Company which has handled so many dead losses recently.

I'm going out with Mark tomorrow evening (he has a date tonight with his pal Gary) so when I finish this letter I'll ring up Roberto and make an appointment for my hair, it'll mean cancelling lunch with Nadia but it can't be helped. I'm afraid she's getting fed up with my ignoring her advice. She won't even let me mention Mark's name which is a bore because I like to talk about him whenever I can! I wonder what your reaction to our friendship would be if you were here now? Even Sally lashed out at me for being such a fool and told me Mark has a wife at home and that I'm wasting my time. I couldn't tell her I knew she was wrong because there was no wife waiting for him in the bungalow when I visited. In any case he's told me the last girlfriend he had and might have married actually jilted him! And he's since got along without anyone else thank you!

The thought of him having been prepared to marry another girl hurts dreadfully but I guess I have to be grateful it didn't come off. He's never mentioned the affair after that little bit of information so I'm none the wiser why he was jilted. I think the girl concerned must be mashigah because he's everything a girl could want in a man. Kind, gentle, amusing, clean, good looking... mind you Norma, he's a bit slow on the love making side. Do you think I'm peculiar to want something a bit more than a mere kiss or his arm around my shoulder? Am I brazen, sinful even? I've done my damnedest to "seduce" him and once thought I was getting somewhere with a really meaty kiss but a rather large lorry parked behind us and the atmosphere was ruined. Any suggestions how I can win him over, or ideas as to why he isn't partial to my overtures?

I wonder if it's (a) because he thinks me physically repulsive! (b) because he suspects – rightly – I'm a virgin! (c) because he's frightened that if he does make love to me, he's be in too deep to avoid matrimony. Take your pick and give me your views when you write. One things for sure, poor old Maurice would give his right arm to have me feel the same about him as I do about Mark!

One encouraging event has been the trip I made to meet his father and sister in Tunbridge Wells. The actual journey could have been quite enjoyable because the countryside looked gorgeous (better than in the States!) and Mark was most attentive, but of course nerves made me feel sick.

Their house isn't anything to write home about; an ordinary semi-detached full of dark furniture and blue and white china on the sideboard, but I guess it does for the old man and Ann. Mr Butler must be in his sixties or older. I'm no good at working out ages. He's bald and blue-eyed and on the whole rather harmless, but Ann was frightfully-frightfully and terrified me from start to finish. We had out the best bone china for tea and there was very polite conversation, the weather, politics, weather, work, summer hols, weather, downfall of the country thru lack of a strong Government, weather... all afternoon I felt like a schoolgirl being interviewed by the Headmistress and I don't think for a sec I was given ten out of ten! I spilt my tea into the saucer, made crumbs on my lap, and while carrying the tea things into the kitchen almost tripped over a stupid rug and to crown it all, damped

my pants because Mr Butler was talking
and I didn't have the pluck to excuse
myself until he had finished – by
which time the damage was done!

I wonder what they think about
Mark being friendly with me. They
asked what my mother and father do and
when I said they had a shop you could
almost see their nose crinkle up with
distaste at the thought of mixing with
someone "commercial", apparently Mr
Butler was in the Civil Service. But
it certainly made me feel queer to
hear darling Mark call Mr Butler
"Dad"; they obviously have a great
affection and respect for each other
which is as it should be between
father and son. You know I'm sure my
Dad would have loved a son. There was
a photograph on the mantelpiece of Mr
and Mrs Butler and I could see Mark
has his mother's straight nose and
same shaped mouth – a gorgeous mouth I
might tell you! But y'know Norma,
being with Mark and his family really
brought it home just how "English" and
"different" they are to us. They don't
seem to have the same warmth and
camaraderie of a Jewish family. Look
how Mark and his sister greeted one
another – they merely shook hands!
They hadn't seen one another for two
months and yet they only shook hands.
Gosh, look at the way our mob behave
when we meet even if we've only been
parted a couple of weeks, a few days

even. We greet each other as if it were centuries!

Although I didn't care for Ann I had to feel sorry for her. Mark had told me about her life on our way there. Apparently her husband had a dreadful accident which left him horribly crippled. He'd fallen asleep during a train journey home and awoken just in time to see he'd reached his station. He quickly jumped out – but, oh pal, he'd opened the wrong door and fallen down onto the rails. He was crippled for years and Ann had to give up her job in the Bank to look after him, and then he died leaving her a very young widow indeed and without any children.

I'm glad your Irvine's family are so sweet and easy, his mother especially sounds a darling. You and my Mum always got on well didn't you? She's an awful fusspot but I wouldn't change her or Dad for the world. I think I would have died myself if I'd lost either one of them like you lost your parents one after the other. Connie's Stan had the same thing happen to him poor thing. Sometimes it's extremely difficult to believe in a God when you hear of such dreadful tragedies. I sometimes get terribly frightened at night when I'm lying in bed thinking of Mark and the future, and wonder if I'm going to be punished for loving him and deceiving Mum and

Dad. I hate going behind their backs but there just isn't any other way. I've told Mark that they don't approve of such friendships but I have a feeling he hasn't realized I'm still keeping quiet about us. Heavens how did I become so serious?

Read out your description of Irvine's house to Mum who said it sounds as if you've fallen on your feet but I told her we mustn't jump to conclusions, just wait patiently for you to be more definite about the situation! Still I'm glad you had Irvine and his family to stay with over Yomtov. Did you get our card in time for Rosh Hashana? Now that the holiday's over the weather is beginning to deteriorate. Yomtov was uneventful this year but at least Nadia and I met afterwards at the Finchley Club, remember how we quarrelled over Isadore last holiday? I say uneventful but there were extra prayers and sermons about Israel. The war may only just be ticking-over but it's still a dreadful thing. I wonder why it's so impossible to get it into the Arabs heads that they're only harming themselves in the long run by being so stubborn? If only they'd join forces with Israel they could have a comfortable, civilized country. These last months the Crescent's been a hub of activity with Mummy and other Jewish inhabitants collecting money

and clothes for the M.D.A., and Mrs
Hammond and her ladies collecting for
the Arab refugees. Just as well we're
all so friendly or there might well be
a cold war amongst ourselves!

Joyce Wood across the road
(British Lion) has just phoned up to
see if I can lend her some money so
she can have her hair done; she's
going to Manchester tomorrow because
Anna Neagle is making a stage
appearance at one of her films. I
don't know if I told you but Joyce is
Anna Neagle's number one fan and will
go simply anywhere to see her, and
she's seen her films a dozen times.
She actually goes up to their flat and
is on very good terms with them, as
least that's what she says. She's a
dreamer but I don't think she'd tell
me fibs. I was over at British Lion
last week and Christine Norden came
into the office. She's really
beautiful. Very made up of course but
slim and elegant. She had some poodles
with her. I wish our firm had some
exciting stars to promote; sometimes I
think Mark is bored or losing heart
with this firm. Gosh I couldn't bear
him to leave...

Well must finish now and phone
the hairdresser. Wonder how to have my
hair done this time? Mummy says she's
fed up with me spending all my cash on
hair-sets and it wouldn't be a bad
idea to give her a rise to help pay

for the phone and electricity bills -
as if it's _my_ fault they're so high.
Connie spends absolutely hours on the
phone to her mates, and has her light
on for ages while she creams and
grooms herself like Lady Dunabunk! I
have to get my hair done often, you
know how ghastly it looks in no time
at all and I must look nice when I go
out with Mark and my fringe is such a
bother. Oh it's all right for those
with naturally curly hair! Perhaps
I'll have my fringe swept away
altogether and ask Roberto to give me
a more mature and sophisticated style.
I'll tell you how I turn out.

Until I hear from you again soon,

God bless,

Lyn.

Coffee Time!

Dear Nadia,

What d'you think you're up to refusing to speak to me? Okay so you feel I've let you down but what I did was because I was frightened you would get into trouble. Don't give me all that stuff about Isadore just wanting a friendly weekend. Do you really think that when it was bedtime you'd both go to a bed of your own? Okay so you are both keen keen keen on each other but if you were pregnant would he still be around for you or away somewhere in Israel?

As for my own double standards you are so right. I've been very wrong getting you to say I was with you when I was with Mark but the difference is that I did always go home – reluctantly of course – to my own bed!

So I'm sorry I've upset you but can we now get over it. I'll do exactly what you say and leave you to make your own mistakes but I hope desperately it won't come to that. I'm getting Billy to bring this down, just scrawl hello on a piece of paper and give it to him to bring back and I'll know everything is o.k. Love, Lyn

Belle dear,

How you are? Yes I know I asked you
that not so very long ago but I'm
asking again! Hope the weather isn't
as lousy as it is here. Is Dovoud
behaving himself and taking good care
of you? How's that tum coming along?
        And do I, dear dear chum, sound
rather unlike my usual cool, calm,
casual self! Well I happen to be
feeling unlike my usual c.c.c. Self
and let me tell you why. But first of
all hold on to your chair or hair
because I don't want you to collapse
in your state of health! Mark and I
are GOING together! Well - as good as
- I think! All right, all right I'll
tell you all about it, let me get my
breath. Mark introduced me to some
more of his friends, a Henry and Iris,
a right crummy pair and I didn't like
them on sight. Anyway we found this
restaurant up West for an evening meal
and we hadn't been there for more than
ten or fifteen minutes when a Jewish
couple took the table next to us. The
man was obviously hemeshe and the
woman was wearing her Kamiah (wish I'd
worn mine might have saved a lot of
trouble but I was wearing a brooch and
bracelet instead and I can't bear too
much stuff on me). When they were

served with soup the man found it cold and told the waiter; the waiter couldn't have cared less so the man asked to see the Head Waiter or Chef. Now he didn't speak loudly or belligerently, and we heard him only because our tables were so close. But Henry, Mark's friend, looked at me with a revolting grin and put a finger to the tip of his nose.

"Trust a yid to make a fuss" he said.

My stomach turned right over I can tell you and my cheeks went hot and cold.

"Nothing wrong with complaining if it's justifiable" I told him. "After all, our soup was also cold, you said so yourself." But he hadn't the pluck to complain!

Not like me to answer back is it, but I was furious.

The wretched man didn't seem to notice how I was feeling because he went on, "Oh they're loud mouthed enough to make a fuss even if everything's A.1, take it from me Marilyn, I know that sort."

Out of the corner of my eye I could see Mark going scarlet and making frantic faces at Henry, but Mr-Know-it-all wasn't taking any notice.

"It wouldn't be a bad idea if the Government thought less about what to do with the coloured and concentrated more on what should be done about them."

"And what do you think should be done about them?" I asked.

"Ship the lot of them back to Palestine" he said.

"Israel" I corrected.

"Palestine, Israel, call it what you like. Perhaps Siberia would be a better place and even that would be too good for them."

Well dearest Belle, what would you have done in my place? Remained in your seat and taken it all with a pinch of salt, or collected your jacket and handbag together and departed? Like I did.

I managed to blurt out, "Excuse me please Mark, I'm going home."

Both Henry and Mark leapt to their feet and Mark said, "For goodness sake Marilyn..." while Henry exclaimed, "What's the matter?"

Mark grabbed me outside the restaurant and told me not to be such an idiot but I said I couldn't possibly stay with his precious friends even if he paid me! He admitted it had been very wrong of Henry to speak so discourteously but he thought I really ought to get rid of that chip on my shoulder. Whereupon I told him, icily I hope, not to bother himself with me any further and I'd see him at the office.

"Stay where you are" he ordered. "I'll just tell them I'm taking you home."

To cut a long story short Belle, I was absolutely heart-broken that he was keeping company with such anti-Semitic people and when I got home – after a silent journey – I decided there was nothing left for me to do but finish with him.

At the office next day he said nothing on the subject, and then after I'd turned down his invitations again and again during the following weeks he suddenly got the message and left me alone. I couldn't sleep or eat I felt so wretched and what made my anguish all the more excruciating was the knowledge that some female was chasing him. First of all she phoned from the North saying she was coming up to London and was he free to meet her? I took the message and phone number for him to ring back and there was no two ways about it he was overjoyed to hear from her. I know for a fact that they did meet and when he spoke to her on the phone a second time in the office he called her "darling".

For days I could hardly eat or sleep and Mum wanted to send me to the doctor for a tonic, but I reckon she would have needed a tonic if she'd known what was upsetting me!

But then came the lunch time when Mark returned to the office and presented me with a gorgeous recording of Beethoven's 1st Piano Concerto which he'd seen in a shop and thought I'd enjoy! Later on that afternoon he announced he was going to Gary and Brenda at the weekend and was I free to go with him?

I went!

But who do you think I find there for the evening? None other than this female from up North, Pauline something or other. She's about Brenda's age but her skin and figure were perfect. She looked as if she'd just stepped out of a bandbox – a Hollywood bandbox! Her nose, eyebrows, cheekbones, mouth, nails and legs … every inch of her exquisitely shaped and groomed. And her hair, red and wavy! And she used to be a singer and a model and apparently Mark met her when she was going in for a Beauty contest promoted by one of the firms he worked for before he came to us. We had cocktails and sandwiches and through the evening other friends came and went; they all knew Pauline and suddenly the penny dropped, he didn't just know her because of his former job, this was the girl Mark had been going with! Once I realized this I hated her more than ever and when it was time for us to go and Pauline shook hands and told me she was delighted to meet Mark's "little friend" I could have scratched her eyes out! And I can't tell you how I felt when she kissed Mark on the mouth and said it wouldn't be long before they met each other again would it?

And so for home and during the drive I took the plunge and asked why Pauline had jilted him. They'd met at this Contest as I've told you and they'd gone together for a long time, sort of unofficially engaged, and everything was fine until she kept on about naming the day and Mark realized he wasn't sure about wanting to be tied yet and was evasive. Pauline had become impatient and huffy, went away on holiday and met the man she married. According to Mark, Pauline and her husband were very happy until a year ago and then got divorced, but that's another story. Except now she's horribly horribly free!

I told Mark I couldn't understand how he'd dithered about marrying such a gorgeous girl and of course I expected him to say it hadn't worried him. But instead he said he couldn't understand it either but we all make mistakes!

I cried all night.

Come Monday morning Mark suggested that if I had some free time I might like to go with him to a furniture store and look at dining room suites????? We went, and when we were looking around the furniture he asked what suite I would choose if I had the chance. For goodness sake what do I know or care about furniture? But when I selected one he actually bought it! I was stunned I can tell you, and more so when he laughed, "All right MY SWEET, you've made your choice now you're stuck with it!"

MY SWEET! I'M stuck with it! So my dearest pal, surely all that behavior implies he has serious intentions toward me, Pauline or no Pauline? No, of course I haven't said a dickey-bird at home, they still don't know I go out with Mark. There'd be ructions if they did. I have to tell them I go out with Brian Levy or Johnny Margolis or Nadia, or that I'm having to stay late at the office for Fanny Adams. I try hard not to think of what their reaction will be should I tell them the truth, for the mo I just want to be happy and contented. Oh Belle I'm sure if you'd stayed over here and got to know Mark better, you would have liked him enormously. He's so genuine and decent. Time is hardly bearable when I'm not with him.

So now you know! Nothing else has happened, I think I've had enough excitement to last me quite a while. As this is a bonus letter pal, I'll expect an extra long one from you but no lectures please! If you luv me like a sister you'll be on my side and wish me as much joy as I wished Dovoud and yourself. Take good care of yourself, you've a very precious person in your tum!

God bless, Lyn

45 Regency Crescent.

Dear Maurice,

Thanks for your letter. Yes, I did see your name in the
J.C., and if I hadn't I would still have known your news
from Sylvie who came flying over here to wave your
letter and newspaper under our nose! Of course I meant
to write and congratulate you but I've been so busy I
haven't found time to do so until now. Muzzletov! It was
a great thrill to read that you'd passed all your exams
with flying colours; I'm sure the States will greet you
with open arms. Before you go I'll give you Norma's
address and Paul's, so that if ever you get near Houston
or Georgia you can drop in and say hello.

     To be quite honest I just can't imagine you being
a Physicist or whatever! It sounds so stuffy and you're
anything but! Yet the way you're going about things it
looks as if you'll get to the top without any trouble.
Sylvie and Ralph are so proud of you.

     Don't worry about Sylvie she'll be o.k. Mummy
says the baby's lying on a nerve and altho it's
uncomfortable it isn't dangerous. I promise to tell you if
there is anything to worry about so you can come flying
home. One thing's for certain, Sylvie's a lot happier now
that you're not in Israel. I don't think she had one night's
good sleep while you were away. I suppose she'll worry
again when you go off to the States but at least she'll
know you'll not be involved in any fighting ..l unless it's
fighting off the girls!

     I stayed at Nadia's last weekend for the first time
in months and had the shock of my life. Nadia told us
that she's thinking of going to Israel – not to work on any
Kibbutz mind you but to see Isadore and his family.
She's been thinking about this for a long time and has

even been writing to him frequently, but not said a word about it to me. I feel very aggrieved, we don't usually keep things from one another. You knew Isadore and Nadia broke it off before he went back didn't you? It was because he told Nad he was staying indoors with some homework but she saw him and the "homework" having coffee together at the Candlelight so that finished that! Once Isadore got home however, he apparently realized how he missed her and wrote to that effect...is this going to be another Belle-and-Dovoud story all over again I wonder? Mr and Mrs Samuel were very subdued, they feel the same way as I do about Nadia leaving the country. Mind you I'd go out there with her if I didn't have someone very special to keep me here in England. Yes, someone very special! Can't tell you anything about him yet except he's marvellous and I hope he feels the same way about me. Sylvie doesn't know anything about him so don't ask her, neither do Mum and Dad, there's a time for everything. Perhaps I'll have something conclusive to tell you when you come home next time.

Until then, once again congrats on being such a clever boy, take care of yourself.

Love,
Marilyn.

Dearest Belle,

Looks as if our letters have crossed.
What a ghastly disappointment. Won't
dwell on the subject in case it starts
you off, but we were all looking
forward to seeing you. But if it can't
be done well that's that, and y'know
perhaps it's all for the best. Bad
weather's arrived with a vengeance,
rain flooding the countryside, farmers
at their wits end, and the employment
situation over here is dreadful. You
should hear Dad on the subject.
Dovoud, for all his skill and ability,
might have an awful time finding a job
and you can't live on love you know -
especially when you've a baby to care
for. Please don't fret or be impatient
… have baby safely and keep on saving.
I know you'll be home before long, you
simply <u>must</u> come!
      A few things have happened since
I last wrote. Sylvie's having a lot of
trouble with her back and Mum says the
baby must be lying on a nerve but
she'll be all right. Doc has ordered
her to stay in bed as much as poss, so
Ralph eats out at lunch time to make
things easier, and Mum, Con and I help
in the evenings. Having Sylvie so
poorly has quite shaken Ralph and he's
fussing around like a mother hen!

Relieved that you're feeling fine and have no problems, see that you keep it that way.

You might be interested to know that Maurice has passed some difficult and special exams which means he can work and study at College in the States. I've given him Norma's address so that he can look her up if he's ever near. I think he goes next February so he'll still be around for his sister's big event. I bet you were surprised to get a note from Norma weren't you? Perhaps now she's done it once she'll carry on, but I doubt it, she's a lousy letter writer and her spelling isn't all that good either!

I could have done without the disappointment of you not coming home. I'm not quite recovered from the shock Nadia gave me recently. Listen to this pal! She might be going to Israel. She and Isadore have been writing to one another for sometime and he wants her to go out and meet his family. You and Dovoud all over again if you ask me! Do you realize if she goes and stays there, I won't have anyone over here at all?

Has Dovoud's brother Roohi come home yet? According to Maurice the fighting in Israel is still very spasmodic and it's the siren more than anything else which is getting the people down. I feel very sorry for the kids having to spend most of the time

down in the shelters. I can remember
very clearly our own war days can't
you, not that it was all that long ago
really. The sickening sound of the
sirens, the frantic rush down the
garden to the shelter, usually
dropping things on the way and getting
a thick ear for being clumsy! Mum
making flasks of tea and mountains of
sandwiches as if we were there for the
duration, and Mrs Hobson with her
bread pudding. And eight of us,
without Dad and Mr Hobson who used to
be homeguarding or fire watching; in
that titchy shelter. How it used to be
suffocating but at least it was safe.
And rotten old Con always keeping the
Girls Crystal to herself so I
shouldn't have it tho I swear she'd
already gone through it a dozen times.
But at least we had no Germans on our
doorstep taking pot-shots at us like
the Israelis have the Arab snipers do
to them. I wonder where my Mark was
during the war? Must ask him some
time.

     We've been to the films and
theatre and I'm really living it up!
Saw Shirley at the weekend but she's
languishing over her absent Rabbi,
still she's doing very well in
business. She's just been promoted to
Buyer and has her own car and smashing
rise. Auntie's worried about her
working so hard but Shirl says she has
to − it's the only way she can keep

her mind off Paul and I know exactly
how she feels!

Well pal, once again take care of
yourself and don't be too harsh with
your In-Laws, you said yourself they
love you, and do remember how hard
your folk tried to keep you over here
with them when Dovoud sent for you.
God bless, see that I hear as soon as
there's any important news!

                    Love from us all,

                            Lyn.

Dear Norma,

Wonderful, wonderful news!
Belle's just had a daughter, 8lbs! She
must have been enormous, and mother
and daughter doing well! She's going
to be called Sharon. Dovoud put a call
through to Mrs Hyam in the middle of
the night, so you can imagine what
chaos there must have been!
I'm writing to you first dear
Norm and then later in the day when
Mark is out I shall get down to a long
letter to Belle. Somehow I've got to
find the words to tell her how I feel.
A daughter. Our Belle a real live Mum.
Incredible and wonderful isn't it?
Please God by you and me! I shall send
her your love and best wishes because
I know you'll be thinking of her and
the baby.
Oh lor, Fanny Adams wants a memo
done straight away so I must finish.
Sal's away again and I've heaps of
work. Don't forget you owe me a
letter.

Love Lyn.

Golden Realm Films.

How's the most beautiful Mum in all the world? And darling Sharon? And I suppose I mustn't overlook the proud dad!

Needn't tell you just how thrilled we were when your Mum phoned first thing to tell us the news. Even Connie who isn't given to being emotional got all wet-eyed along with me! Hope hospital wasn't as uncivilized as you feared, and that you didn't have a bad time with Sharon; Sylvie said she'd forgotten how ghastly it all was! Doesn't give me much encouragement! I won't nag you to write because you'll be busy enough getting used to dealing with a baby, only as soon as you do find a spare moment please put pen to paper and tell me all the news. Oh how I'd love to see Sharon! Who does she look like? As both Dovoud and yourself are dark and curly haired I reckon it'll be hard to tell. Sharon's such a pretty name. Your Mum told me it's after her mother and she really wanted Sarah but you didn't like that. Promise not to laugh pal, but I've been knitting a matinee coat for ages but the endless times I've had to unpick it and start again! I really think I'll have to give up and buy something off the peg otherwise Sharon won't get anything until next Chanukah!

I'm seeing Nad this lunch time and she'll be thrilled with the news. If I go down to her at the weekend (Mark might go and see his Dad) we'll pop round to your house and see how they're taking the news. If I know your Mum she'll be having everyone in to drink to you and the baby.

Now let me tell you about Sylvie and her infant who arrived two days ago. It's a little girl, 5lbs, healthy and Sylvie's fine but she said she had a bad time. The baby's called, wait for it, Tracy Zoe Wanda Bettina! Forgot to ask your Mum if she's putting Sharon's arrival in the J.C., I'll have to look out on Friday. Incidentally, went down to Contracts and told them about Sharon. Mr Goodman sends his best wishes and "many happy returns"!

Mark knows I'm typing this letter despite the pile of work (tons of trade shows and Premières) and he's highly amused at my delight. If only I could have a daughter, his daughter of course – or son for that matter. Just as long as it's his! Everything's very cosy between us only he hasn't said what his intentions are for the future and I'm frightened to say too much on the subject because he got all narky

with his first girlfriend because she
went on rather a lot about settling
down. I don't want to nag him and
perhaps drive him away. Guess I'll
have to be patient and hope for the
best!

Well, God bless the three of you,
<u>three</u> of you, doesn't that read well?
Take good care of each other and
please write just as soon as you can.

Lyn. AUNTIE Lyn!

Hi there dear Belle, how's everything going with mummy daddy and baby??? How I'd love to see you feeding Sharon and bathing her … does Dovoud help and I wonder what part your In-Laws take in caring for their granddaughter. Rachmaninoffs 2nd piano concerto is playing on 3 as I write … I hope you get the BBC3 or Persian equivalent and listen to it with Sharon.

I don't know whether I should tell you about something creepy and inexplicable …

One of our visitors calling in to see Dickie is a Jewish man, Walter Dorfman, he writes a column for a variety of papers and has used Dickie for information about what is going on in Wardour Street. Well Dickie's not here any more. I did tell you this didn't I? So Walter's latched on to me. He knows I enjoy writing so we chat about what we're working on and he's told me about his latest project. This is where the creepy comes in! He's writing about the experiences of a 17th century Catholic Lord Nithsdale, who is imprisoned in the Tower of London for a variety of reasons I can't remember now … the point is, this is a <u>first person</u> saga because Walter is getting Nithsdale's experiences from the horses mouth via the help of a Spiritualist!

I think my expression must have been one of disbelief while I was listening to him because Walter invited me to go with him to Caxton Hall where the spiritualist Mr Harris has his room. I dithered about whether I should go or not but Walter said all I had to do was take down notes and listen! This Mr Harris turned out to be a short, round man with a soft gentle voice, very polite when I was introduced.

So listen to this! Mr Harris was relating all that was happening to him as a prisoner when he suddenly stops and turns to me. "You enjoy writing don't you Marilyn?" I said yes and he says, "Well you'll have to be patient, you will have some success when you are forty!"

Then almost in the same breath he carries on with his imprisonment in the tower, Lord Nithsdale's fear of not being pardoned and ultimately being executed!

Then once again Mr Harris turned to me, "You have a personal problem, Marilyn." I wasn't impressed at his perception, after all most of us have a problem or two, but wait dear Belle, he had more to say.

"You have a relationship with a man who has lost his wife." Oh Belle I thought my heart was going to leap out of my body! "And you are worrying in case she will feel betrayed … be assured my dear, this lady is extremely joyful that her husband is finding happiness with someone who loves him deeply."

Now Belle let me tell you emphatically that no way could he know about Mark. Walter couldn't have told him anything because he didn't know about us, we never discussed our personal lives, only spoke of what we had read and written about, the films Golden Realm and other film companies were producing. And then to practically finish me off Mr Harris said, "His wife died from TB ... " A pause and then "Her name is Jane." His words sort of echoed in my ears. "Is Jane." And he was right! Mark's wife was Jane! I know I've never mentioned that Mark is a widower, I only learnt about it myself a while ago when I was at his home and we were talking about (oh gorgeous, they're playing Bruch … exquisite!) holidays and families and Mark suddenly looked at me very searchingly and I thought 'oh now what?'

And he said … "I haven't told you I lost my wife from TB. It was during the war." Oh no, he'd belonged to someone else! What sort of person am I Belle to think only of myself … how could I be jealous of someone who had died. I wanted to put my arms around him and say I was sorry for this tragedy but not to worry because here I was for him. Of course I was tearful and he wiped my eyes and said he should have told me much earlier but he hadn't expected us to become so close.

It was quite late when Walter and I parted and needless to say I hardly slept a wink that night and I still go over the situation even now. How did Mr Harris know about Mark and his wife? How could he actually be this Lord Nithsdale, a 17th century Catholic imprisoned in the Tower of London? Before I left Walter he told me that Nithsdale's wife had come to the Tower and dressed him in her clothes and they walked free to catch a boat and escape to France … or was it Italy, I'm not sure now. I wish there was someone I could ask about spiritualism and healing and so on but I doubt whether a Rabbi would want to ponder over such a subject.

Of course one thought in the night leads to another … not only had I not known Mark had been married but I know nothing about his time in the war. While I was an evacuee he was a young sailor for goodness sake, he could have been drowned! Oh Belle there is still plenty I don't seem to know about him.

OK, now for news from home – Mark and I are still o.k. I missed him so much on holiday - he's mentioned that he has plans for us but what? Your guess is as good as mine, could be concerts, a weekend in a cosy hotel or even just being together in the bungalow would be heaven, but whatever I do presents the problem of deceiving Mum and Dad again which I really hate doing, and loads of times I end up with a splitting headache from the worry! No, I still haven't let on to Mark that no one knows about our relationship, he might get it into his head that being underhand is not right, he's

a very upright man. Man! That is why I love him, he is so different to all the boys I've been out with. He takes me seriously, makes me feel safe. No silly games …
although I wouldn't mind a little show of desire on his part! I wonder just how long I have to wait before he realizes we are made for each other! And how am I ever going to tell Mum and Dad that I want to marry someone who isn't Jewish?

Nothing new from Norma, she's still enjoying Irvine and his family, they're obviously rich and Irvine has a superb apartment in the better part of Houston, and being close to the family home he's there Friday nights taking Norma with him. She's a bit worried that sooner or later she is going to be asked to light the Shabbas candles and she doesn't want to make a mess of that. Oh just putting this down makes me wonder what will I do if I actually marry Mark … will he understand that a Jewish wife must welcome in the Sabbath just like my Mum does. Oh bother, have to call it a day dear pal, Dad has just put his head around the door and asked how are they expected to sleep with this machine chattering away!

So loads of love, write soon.

Lyn

Home.

Dearest Belle, here I am again!

Hope everything is o.k. with the f-a-m-i-l-y!! Saw the photos you sent your Mum and Sharon is absolutely the image of you round and curly and can't wait to hold her!

I thought I'd tell you ever so briefly about the hols abroad. We were absolutely mad to go and don't ask me why we did because I can't tell you. How much pleasure can you enjoy when you are practically unconscious from sunstroke? Or you walk miles and miles without a rest and food because there's a big sister bossing us about all the time! I shall never understand Connie wanting to go on holiday and leaving Stan behind. Mind you the south of France is heavenly but only if you travel there by comfortable transport and stay in one of the luxurious hotels with good food, soft beds, swimming pool and spa.

Lying in bed thinking I was going to die from sunstroke – we'd been so stupid and stayed in the sun too long – I kept Mark in my mind as much as I could, going over our times together, the way he can be so caring … and I thought of Mum and Dad as well of course but that brought the guilt and I thought this was why I was being punished! But in the end all was o.k. we had a fantastic time in Paris and the journey home was fine. Is there anything you need and how good is the post when there is a parcel because both Nad and I have something for Sharon and we wouldn't want it to get lost. Can't wait for her to be old enough for a doll, in fact I'm half inclined to buy one now and keep her in my bedroom!

Being serious for a moment don't you think you ought to see a doctor about the way you're feeling – although I think he will say it's because of all you went through having Sharon and not having your own family around at such an important time. Why don't you speak to Dovoud's mother now that you have some Farsi, she has always sounded such a lovely lady. No of course I wouldn't say a word to your Mum in any case I'm sure everything will be o.k. very soon.

Connie is yelling for me to help tidy up the kitchen so better do as I'm told!

Much love,

Lyn

Oh Norma what am I going to do? I wish you weren't so far away ... I need someone to talk to and tell me what to do. Nadia's no help, she won't even let me mention Mark's name.

The thing is I left GR a month ago. Only a month? It seems an eternity. Do you know why I had to leave? Because my sister told me to! You see Mum asked me what my plans were for the weekend and I told her the truth. Me and my big mouth! Usually I'd say I was meeting Nadia or one of the boys I know but suddenly desperately wanted to tell the truth. I was going to a concert with Mr Butler!

Mum's mouth fell open, she went very white and then she almost screamed, "You'll do no such thing".

Why?" as if I didn't know. Mum was really white, "Do I have to tell you why? Have you gone mad?" then Connie came rushing upstairs yelling, "What's the matter? What's going on?"

Mummy said, "Your clever sister here's going out with a yok. Ever heard of such a thing?"

Poor Connie looked as if she'd been struck by lightning then she got hold of me and shook me yelling, What d'you think you're playing at? Have you lost your mind?"

Then there was the three of us sobbing and yelling. I told them I loved Mark and he was a marvellous man and they'd see that when they met him ..... then Connie had to rush into the bathroom and get a wet flannel to put on Mum's face because she looked as if she was going to pass out. Connie made Mum sit on the edge of my bed and cuddled her but Mum just went on crying. Then Connie lunged at me and slapped my face and I rushed out of the house over to Sylvie and asked if I could use her phone. Of course she got all het up at the state of me and I wouldn't tell her what was wrong but she heard everything I said to Mark about not meeting him and so I had to tell her what was the matter and she was as horrified as Mum and called Maurice down to "talk some sense" into me but I rushed out before he appeared.

I walked round and round the block wondering what to do but it was so cold I had to go home. When I'd told Mark on the phone what had happened – he wanted to know why I was crying – he said, "Do you mean to tell me they still don't know we are going out together? For heavens sake don't upset them any more, we'll discuss this on Monday."

I was dreading a scene when I got back because Dad should have been in by then but Connie grabbed me as I came into the house and made me promise not to say a word to Dad. She and Mum had decided to keep schtum about it hoping to make me see the light before the weekend was out. I told Connie I'd never change my mind about Mark but was willing to listen to what she and Mum had to say. Talk about Inquisition! When I got to bed in they marched demanding to know "just how long has this been going on?" So I told them, I told them all I know about Mark and his family (not that his father was a church warden!) and how much he means to me. I couldn't bear it.

Mum was absolutely heartbroken. She sat on the bed crying, Connie was crying – and I was crying. The weekend was hell, Mummy went about the house like a ghost and Connie looked as if she could murder me. Only Dad, who didn't know what was going on and dear Stan were civil to me. Mind you I spent most of the time upstairs because I couldn't stop crying. By the time the weekend was over I knew I couldn't bear to see Mum in such a state, she was making herself ill. I was making her ill!

"You've got to leave that job" ordered Connie, "and get some sense into your head."

So that's what I did. I went in early and saw Mrs Friel and told her I had to leave for personal reasons. I spent an age in the loo before I could go upstairs because I was such a wreck and I just had to stop crying before seeing Mark.

When I more or less tottered into the office Mark was already there but so was Harry Price of Galaxy Blocks so we couldn't discuss anything and I had such a lot of work and a blinding headache. When he was free and I told him what had happened at home Mark said: "For the life of me I can't see what all the fuss is about but you were wrong to keep it from them in the first place." And then the phone rang and would you believe it, it was my Mum! Mark listened and said, "I'm sorry you feel like this Mrs Ash, I'm extremely fond of Marilyn and have only her welfare at heart." Then he listened some more and said, "If that is how you feel" his face was so grim, "I quite understand. Please don't worry any longer."

When he'd put the phone down he told me, "That was your Mother and she's asked me to make sure you have given in your notice and to promise I won't see you again after you have left. As it's for your own good I must do as she asks."

I was furious! With Mum and yet in despair for her ... furious with Mark because he seemed willing to let me go without a fight. I told him I had already given in my notice but that it didn't mean we couldn't see each other when all the excitement had died down. In fact what we could do now that they knew about us is to go home together and they would see how much we cared for one another. But he wouldn't listen to me. "Your parents obviously feel very strongly about a friendship with someone not of your Faith and I see no point in causing them any further anxiety." Then without another word, no gesture to comfort me, he got on with his work.

Not once Norma, not once during that morning did he show any concern at what had happened or the fact I had to keep on disappearing to hide my crying. When he was going out to have lunch I asked him whether he cared at all that we might not see each other again. He just shrugged, "Perhaps it's all for the best, in fact I'm sure it is."

I guess it sunk in then, I obviously wasn't as important to him as he was to me. I'd taken too much for granted, been living in a dream. I'd thought he cared a lot, perhaps enough for marriage, but he'd really had no such ideas. Perhaps he'd even been waiting for such a situation to come up so he could wash his hands of me before we got in too deep. Yet Norm, I could swear he cared! Why else take me out, take me to meet his friends and family? It wasn't because he wanted anything from me I know, he was always very very proper ... if he'd been leading me up the garden path wouldn't he have taken advantage of me? There were enough times when I was ready, willing and able.

There was no way I could work the week out so when Mark left for lunch I stuffed as much as I could in my bag put some finished letters on his desk, stood there in tears until Sally came in and said she was coming with me to the station. I was so wretched Norm if Sally hadn't been there to keep hold of me I think I would have fainted.

I had to look for another job quickly because at home everyone acted like warders! You've seen the address up top. I got the job despite looking like a wreck and no references to show my employer but of course they've been in touch with Personnel who obviously reassured them I was capable of being an experienced secretary. Not a bad job, the boss is young and pleasant. Younger than Mark and far more easy going but I don't want him, I want Mark back. Sorry I'm being such a wet blanket.

I'm taking it for granted you are o.k. Tell me what's been happening in the USA. I wonder what reaction there would be if I decided to come over to you? Would it be easy to find a job and a place to live? It was easy for you wasn't it because you were with your family. I really am thrilled the Deli is so successful.

Cheerio pal, love you lots.

Lyn.

Dearest Maurice,

So good to hear from you and what a darling you are
to be thinking of me when you should be
considering all the wonderful things you're going to
do over there in the States! Glad the journey was
such fun but what, no shipboard romances to report
on? I'm surprised at you! I've written to Norma
telling her you have her address and I'm sure she'll
be delighted to fix you up with a suitable dame to
show you the sights.
　　　Life hasn't altered much during the weeks
you've been gone. Sylvie still hasn't forgiven me for
causing such chaos at home. She's very cold and
doesn't even ask me to look after the kids. I don't
know if she thinks I'm going to lead them astray or
something; as if you could make Jon-Jon do
anything he doesn't want to do! Connie's been a
right bore about it all, glaring at me all the time and
very sharp tongued, but Stan's sweet and
understanding. Mind you his sweetness hurts even
more because he reminds me so much of Mark. Now
what would have been the good of telling you about
him, you'd only have read the riot act like everyone
else! And thanks for being keen on me "despite
everything" (mind you, you make me sound as if I've
got leprosy!) and I shan't forget how kind you were
during the whole "escapade". I promise to do as you
ask; if you aren't fixed up by the time you come
home and I'm still free, I'll think about us going out
together. Did you ever meet Brian Levy, he works

down Wardour St., well he's been phoning home to see how I am and ask me out but I've got no inclination to see anyone.

My cousin Judy came down for a long weekend and we cried on each others shoulder. Me because of Mark, her because she's so fed up at home. My Zaida lives with them and he's very ill and it casts a gloom over the household as you can imagine and Judy says its like living in a morgue. Of course she loves Zaida but she says the worry makes her Mum and Dad edgy and she doesn't seem to be able to do anything right for them. Judy's been a real brick, no scolding or recriminations from her like I get from Connie and Nadia. Oh everyone at Brighton knows about my "downfall" and Judy says her Mum and Dad were really cut up about it because they're so fond of me, and if ever she got it in her head to go with a gentile they'd murder her! I'm sure once she's twenty one she'll be out of the house like a shot, and I reckon I'll be leaving home too if things go on the way they are.

Can hear your Sylvie downstairs, she's come in for coffee having left Ralph with Jon-Jon and Tracy. Tracy is absolutely gorgeous but can she yell, you can hear her from the end of the street. Do you realize she will be toddling by the time you come back to us? Thanks again for your sympathy and advice, I'll write and tell you how I get on. Take care and have fun on the campus, and should you ever see Norma give her a big kiss for me.

Affectionately,
Marilyn.

Dearest Belle, you get the silliest ideas! Why on earth should I be <u>broigus</u> with you? I simply haven't written as much as usual because I've been in the depths of despair and you're the last person I wanted to worry because you've got Sharon to cope with.

But now you've asked what's wrong I'm going to tell you. For a start you can see the new address and perhaps realize I've left Golden Realm – and Mark. Briefly Mum found out about him, or rather I told her, and so we've had to break up. Mark obviously wasn't bothered about it and that's that. I left Golden Realm for the firm above and Mark and I haven't seen one another for months. Don't create because I didn't tell you – you see I thought Mark loved me and would go out of his way to make Mum and Dad see it could work out for us, but apparently I was wrong. He didn't even make an effort to see Mum and Dad at all or suggest we gave each other a rest until things calmed down and then start again. Oh Belle, I can't tell you how unhappy I am. I cry myself to sleep, I don't feel like eating or doing anything. Living seems pointless, there's nothing to look forward to.

Maurice turned out a real brick and was very consoling but he didn't stay around for long because he went to the States to take up his place in College. Sylvie isn't too nice to me because she's very fond of Mum and it worried her terribly to see Mum so cut up over me. Incidentally, Dad doesn't know about Mark – he thinks I left Golden Realm because I squabbled with Fanny Adams.

Don't let's think about it any more.

Did I ever tell you Nadia was thinking of going to Israel to be with Isadore? Thank goodness that idea didn't materialize. To Mr and Mrs Samuel's relief and mine too I can tell you, she fell for an absolutely wonderful boy, Mick Wise, who she met at the Starlight Rooms and it quite looks as if this could be the real thing. Yet I know it's been the real thing for Nadia ever since we've known her, but if I tell you she actually goes to classical concerts with Mick you'll appreciate he must be something special. And he's such a contrast to Nadia, he's quiet and calm and seems to take everything in his stride while our Nad is like a cat on hot bricks. I'll be perfectly happy if she's serious over him because at least he's English and Jewish! And will keep her in this country. As for Isadore, for all we know he's still pining in Israel, poor boy.....well someone has to lose, and I should know.

Shirley and Paul are still writing to one another but the family wish they weren't. Paul's letters are so full of grisly details that Shirley's almost a nervous wreck. Quite bad enough we can read newspaper reports about the black-and-white battles in the South without her getting firsthand information from someone she loves, and Paul makes no bones about willing to risk life and limb to promote peace between the races!

In Norma's last letter, besides commiserating with me, she described her new flat and new boyfriend. He sounds nice enough, a kind, wholesome yank, yes Jewish, but not as interesting as Irvine. I wonder what was behind their breaking up. Norma said they parted best of friends but didn't elaborate further. I was astonished because she'd been taken home tons of times and apparently thought the world of his family. Perhaps she's harbouring some heartbreak too but isn't such a crybaby as me.

You might be interested to know Sam and Freda are expecting their first and Freda is looking really pretty. A shame she hasn't "changed"; I know this is making Auntie and Uncle very unhappy and spoiling the pleasure of their first grandchild. At least my Mum and Dad wouldn't have had to worry on this score if I'd married Mark. Our kids would have been Jewish.

On the subject of happiness, I'm sure you and Dovoud must be perfectly content with your lot and I'm truly thrilled for you. I'm sorry I've neglected the letter writing recently but it hasn't been because I've not cared how you're all getting along, you know that. I'm sure you can see how miserable I am and will be patient with me in the future if I don't write quite as often as I used to. This job isn't too bad but not as much fun as Golden Realm. Oh no, I'm starting again.

Thrilling to hear of Sharon's progress. Tracey's pushing herself up too, has lots of hair and Ralph thinks there's no baby in the world as beautiful as his! I don't want to be disloyal to Sylvie but I bet Sharon beats hers hands down! Love to Dovoud and a big very big kiss to Sharon.

Take care of yourselves,

Lyn.

Melody House.

My very dearest Belle, such wonderful wonderful news! Everything's all right. Mark and I have made it up and Mum and Dad have given us their blessing. Well it's given reluctantly as you can imagine but we've got it and that's all that matters. Oh Belle I can't believe it, and I'm so deliriously happy!

It happened yesterday. Melody House isn't far from Foyles and I spent some lunchtimes there and you know Foyles isn't too far from Golden Realm and I had this terrible terrible ache just to see the place. Yes perhaps it was piling on the agony but I was also hoping to convince myself there'd be no reaction once I got there, that I'd find I'd got over wanting Mark. Well of course I hadn't, when I arrived outside G.R. it was agony and I longed to have just a glimpse of him. But Mark didn't come out of the building, nothing as convenient as that, but dear Billy did and was overjoyed to see me, bless him, and was bursting with news. Barbie's Fanny Adam's right hand girl (they deserve each other!) Sally is going out with a chap from another Film Company. Fanny Adams was on holiday, and Mark out at lunch.

'Why don't you go in and see Sally?" he suggested.

I wiped my eyes and obliged. Nothing's changed. Barbie's still vile, big-headed now as well as big-breasted, and Sally's still coping with the Charmer but now she's found a chap. So happy for her because she's a dear girl and she'd had a rotten time with her mother who had to go into a Nerve hospital. Although I knew Mark wasn't in his office I had to peep in. my successor's desk was absolutely tidy, not an item out of place – things <u>had</u> changed after all! Of course I nearly started blubbing again! Well I was standing there dazed with longing when Sally yelled, "Heyho, here's Butler, steady on Lyn!"

She scuttled out as Mark came in but my legs wouldn't budge. Honestly, it was as if my feet were glued to the floor. Belle darling, he <u>was</u> glad to see me! He was astonished and pleased, I saw the expression with my own two eyes. For a moment I thought he was going to get hold of me but the very next second he looked as cool as ice.

"Well look who's here. How are you keeping?" as if I was one of his customers in for a block or campaign book.

I don't know even now how I found the voice to tell him I was keeping well, to ask after his own health, and to tell him – in case he was interested - where I was working. But before I could summon up enough pluck to ask if he'd missed me at all, his new girl came in. and I left. I was in a daze. I couldn't stop crying. Did people look at me? Why haven't I any control over my behaviour? Needless to say I could hardly do a stroke of work all yesterday afternoon and Mr Plummer, my boss, wasn't at all pleased with me. How could I concentrate when all I could see was Mark's beloved face? By the time work was nearly finished I was half demented with unhappiness and had made up my mind to borrow some money from somewhere to come out to you! And then, oh joy, just before hometime there was a telephone call for me. Mark! He wanted to know if I could keep myself busy for another twenty minutes and if so he'd finish his work and come and pick me up – if I wanted him to! Just like that … I was absolutely delirious with happiness. Talk about extremes. One moment down in the depths, the next my cup runneth over! Mr Plummer must have thought me completely mad the way I scrabbled around for my toilet stuff so I could tidy myself up for Mark. That took some doing. My nose and my eyes were so red and sore but when we eventually met, Mark just took me in his arms and kissed me.

"We'll find somewhere to eat and talk things over."

Talk? We didn't stop talking. About what we'd been doing without one another, and how all afternoon after our surprise meeting he'd been trying to get me out of his mind – and couldn't! Belle, he really and truly loves me. But why didn't he try and keep me when Mum kicked up a row?

"It's wrong to come between parents and child" Mark explained. "I couldn't do it. Besides, I was sure it wouldn't be long before we'd forget each other." But he'd made a mistake.

We finished our meal and then he said I must phone home and tell them he was bringing me in the car. I felt sick with terror.

I got through to Connie and told her, there was an absolutely stony silence, then I heard her speaking to someone and some shouting. I waited ages and then Daddy got on the line.

"Are you out of your mind? What do you want to do, break your mother's heart?"

I told Daddy we couldn't discuss it properly over the phone and Mark wanted to speak to him and Mummy. He shouted he didn't want to see Mark; that if I didn't come home immediately he'd break every bone in my body! Then Stan took over and said, "Are you sure you know what you're doing

Marilyn? All right, bring him home. I'll talk to Mum and Dad."

Oh Belle I was so scared when I took Mark indoors and he looked just as worried. I love him all the more for going through this bother over me especially when he can't comprehend what all the fuss is about. Well Mum and Dad were civilized in the circumstances. No threat to cast me out of their lives for ever; no order never to darken their doors again or threat to sit Shiva if I married Mark. It has happened in Orthodox families I know. Oh God, what would I have done if they'd said such awful things?

When Connie and I went into the kitchen to make some tea I asked her what she thought of Mark. She shrugged, "He seems harmless enough, but why on earth you couldn't find yourself someone Jewish beats me!" and then proceeded to cry!

I think Mum and Dad were asking Mark about his family while I was out of the room, and when I eventually went back they all looked pale and strained. Mark wouldn't have any tea but said he ought to go home. I went with him to the car but as Daddy and Stan were in the doorway I felt too shy to kiss Mark goodnight – but I'm going to make up for it this evening when we meet to celebrate.

When he'd left I asked Mum and Dad what they thought about him. Should have kept my mouth shut. Mum started crying again and Daddy just shrugged and said he seemed a decent enough man but ... and then his eyes filled and I got all choked up and went to bed.

So now, reluctant as they are, Mum and Dad have accepted the situation and I know Mark won't disappoint them; he's every bit as kind, gentle and stable as Connie's Stan. Of course I phoned Nadia first thing this morning to tell her the news and it hurts like the dickens not to have her share my joy or wish me luck. She just said, "Well it's your life chum."

Yes, my life – to spend with Mark. Not immediately of course, but sometime in the future. We've made no definite plans but the heavenly prospect is there. I'd marry him tomorrow if he asked but I must be patient. It's only fair to let Mummy and Dad get used to the idea of Mark, and to let Mark get used to the idea of me!

Belle darling, you are happy for me aren't you? I guess your In-Laws being so religious will be horrified to hear that your pal is marrying "out"! But you see, I feel it can't be so terribly wrong or the Almighty wouldn't let it happen. Deep down I know it doesn't matter. Mark's such a good person and this is the main thing isn't it?

Must finish now Mr Plummer's buzzing for me. He's less patient than my Mark and no sense of humour whatsoever. Much love to Dovoud and Sharon and write soon. I'm so happy!

God bless ,

Lyn.

Dearest Norma,

A brief but wildly happy letter – for a change! Just
want to tell you all's well between Mark and myself
and we have everyone's blessing to be friends. Hard
come by with lots of tears and heartache I can tell
you but we've got it all the same.

Very briefly this is how it happened. I
succumbed to visiting Golden Realm, saw Mark, he
appeared to be quite unconcerned at seeing me
again and of course I was absolutely wretched with
despair. But, oh I still can't believe it, during the
afternoon he phoned to say he was coming to get me
and it turned out that he's missed me dreadfully but
didn't feel he had any right to make trouble between
Mum and Dad and me. He said all the time we'd
been apart he'd been telling himself he didn't care,
and even after he saw me again he was determined
not to let it matter, but in the end he decided he
couldn't lose me!

Aren't I the luckiest girl in the world? We
celebrated, just us two, at the first restaurant we
ever went to together and I'd felt ill from the
excitement and an unkoshered steak! We've also
been to his friends Brenda and Gary to celebrate
and they really seem to like me and Brenda wants to
know when we're getting engaged, but that's the
rub, Mark says that in the circumstances – Mum
and Dad's feelings towards him – we shouldn't rush
into anything. So what it amounts to is that we're
unofficially engaged but I've a marvellous feeling

that he's going to get me a ring to prove everything is on the level!

Although I've not mentioned it before I have wondered what went wrong between Irvine and yourself. There didn't seem to be any complications with that relationship and you were getting so chummy with his family. Do you really like this Stephen more? Oh I'm so deliriously happy I want everyone, especially my dearest pals, to be as happy! Belle's letters are full of Sharon as you can imagine. She's got curly hair and dimples, weighs a ton, and according to Mrs Hyam who has photos, looks just like Belle did as a baby! I can't wait for Belle to bring the baby home to see for ourselves.

Have you had a note or phone call from Maurice? He did promise to contact you while he was over there. I've had one letter since he arrived in the States, but I'll have to write soon and put him in the picture about Mark and me because he thinks it's all over and said that if I was free when he came back and he wasn't tied up we ought to go together!

Well dear friend, that's all for now. I've a pile of work for Mr Plummer and unlike Mark he insists nothing is left over to the next day. When I first met him I thought he was o.k. but actually he's an absolute bore and I don't know that I'll be able to stick him much longer. There are two other Directors and they're not half as bad but they've already got girls. I wish I could go back to Golden Realm but Mark's satisfied with my replacement the rotter, and the only vacancy is in Contracts and I wouldn't work there if it was the last job on earth.

You will write soon won't you and don't forget to congratulate me, no sour words thank you! And start saving to come over for the wedding … my legs have gone all weak at the thought of it, and I can't wait, oh I can't wait! To be with Mark always!

All my love,

Lyn.

Hi there dear Judy!

I just have to write and say sorry for all the hassle last weekend. I knew I shouldn't have come but your Mum said it would do us both good. Well it didn't do us good did it! Yes I know it was alright when we were out and away from the house, we could relax and let our hair down but indoors with your Dad it was murder. I thought if he had one more go at me about Mark I would scream, pack up and go home. It was only because of you and darling Zaida that I bit my tongue and stayed ... until Sunday's slanging match.

Why do you all think I'm not miserable at giving my Mum and Dad such a bad time? It hurts me more than I can say when I see their misery. When I came home from work yesterday I found Mummy sitting in the lounge. Just sitting there staring ahead, her eyes and cheeks wet. No lights on, just sitting ... and in her nightie! I put my arms around her, she was cold and trembly. I didn't ask what was wrong, why hadn't she gone to the shop, why wasn't she dressed. I know the answer ... and I can't help her. I brought down a cardigan and her dressing gown and made us some tea. She couldn't hold the teacup, her hand was shaky. I'm really worried about her but what can I do?

Please don't start on me ... I can't give Mark up. Mum and Dad, Connie and everyone else have got to see that this is my life, I could well be doing the wrong thing but that's the chance I want to take. I sat there cuddling Mum and telling her Mark knew all about Jewish things and I would never ever forget who I was and he was just like Daddy principled and honest and so on and so on ... and then I took her upstairs and washed her face and combed her hair and persuaded her to put on a dress ... and then we went down and I asked Mum if I should fry some fish for when Dad came in ... I knew that would get her going because as usual she told me I didn't know the first thing about frying fish so find the matzo meal, get out the egg, and leave the rest to her!

But I feel there are going to be other times when she is going to be low and Daddy not much better. As for your Mum and Dad I love them very much but not enough to put up with their harsh attitude. I'm amazed really that they are letting you keep in touch with me but then you have a mind of your own and I reckon they know we would never let each other down. Would we?

The boss is hovering close by so that's your lot. Big kisses for Zaida, he's more important than all of us put together so I hope he gets better very soon.

All my love

Lyn

Howdy dear Norma!

Here I am again! Been thinking of you a lot because a bevy of American tourists were interviewed outside Buckingham Palace for their opinion on the Coronation! I looked hard and long at the crowd but you weren't amongst them! You did watch the event didn't you? Did you feel homesick perhaps as the cameras moved through the streets of London? Don't forget that if you want to come HOME my bed is still big enough for us both, I haven't put on any weight since you went away, and the bath water is as hot as ever! It still makes me smile to remember how you and Belle used to love coming to me so you could have a bath and I loved going to you so that I could go to the Turkish baths! Yes I know, the grass is always greener.

Well the Coronation was a wonderful day, all the shops and offices had closed down but the bosses entered into the spirit of the occasion and allowed staff to take over every window and balcony to see the celebrations going on in the streets, marching bands, guides and scouts and other groups with flags and banners and in most towns street parties. I was in seventh heaven because Mark took me to a club in Regent Street where all the film people and writers and artists congregate. I don't remember much about who I met only that as there was a shortage of chairs, I sat on Mark's lap and terrifically happy to do so. It was really wonderful because he knew tons of people and he was actually showing everyone that I was most definitely with him! I did wonder if his friend Valerie from British Lion was there and she might see us together and realize we're a couple!

The Queen looked absolutely fantastic. Her dress was in satin, pearls and diamanté, designed as expected by Norman Hartnell who has always made her wardrobe. Ii looked good of course but too fussy for my wedding dress! I couldn't help wondering how she felt about the life ahead of her and probably sad that it took losing her Dad to put her in this position. I wonder how Philip felt suddenly attached to a Queen. When we see them together – well it isn't really together because he's always a few steps behind her – they looked happy enough. A magazine article said that walking behind men is the normal thing in Persia, men rule women submit. I must ask Belle if that is true. In her last letter she asked if you miss the excitement of Wardour Street and how far are you from Hollywood and what's the Jewish community like? Do you ever go to shul – just remembered a Synagogue is called Temple where you are isn't it? And she's learning Farsi which will help her enormously.

Mark surprised me by remarking that the Queen had looked good in her army uniform – they were showing snippets of her life on the tv – and I said how most evacuees, me included, had wished we were older so the yanks and even the itys would be interested in us. That night once I was tucked up in bed and going over the evening again and again! I realized that Mark must be even older than I thought because while I was evacuated with Mum and Connie, Mark was in the merchant navy and torpedoed! I don't know if he was married then or that was still to come. Such a lot I don't know about him, he doesn't offer any information about his life and I'm frightened to ask him in case he starts to feel trapped – have I told you that was what happened with his last girlfriend – she got too possessive and Mark had second thoughts about marrying her and that was the end of that affair, thank goodness!

I've been writing this while everyone is out of the office but I can hear voices coming closer so better stop. They aren't as tolerant as Mark. Don't let me wait too long for your letter because as you know I have to share your news with Belle. Oh yes, Nadia sends her love.

Lyn.

Hi dear Norm,

So pleased you saw and enjoyed the Coronation, do you think a high percentage of the community were interested? Apparently there were tons of Canadians in the crowds; I don't know that we could tell one from another, everyone had flags and a variety of hats and tiaras! I bet the Yanks would love a royal family of their own but I can't think of any American politician or family who would be as classy can you? Mind you what do I know about politics home or abroad! Whenever there is the next Presidential election are you allowed to have a say or do you have to wait for a certain amount   of years? Yes it was a gorgeous dress when you could see it uncovered by the red robes etc. and no not my idea of a wedding dress! Oh Norm I've gone all shivery thinking of it even though there's no chance of getting married for absolutely ages. Connie and Stan come first and my worry is that Mark will have tons of time to change his mind!

At last he's told me more about Jane his late wife. They were both in their twenties and Mark was in the merchant navy and she was a Wren. I bet they made a super looking couple not that I've seen a photo of her. That's what I've always found strange in Mark's home no photos! At least not downstairs, I did peep into his bedroom and saw some framed photos on a dressing table but I didn't have the pluck to go and look up close. And I've had no invitation from Mark to go into his bedroom! Anyway they only had three years together and then she caught TB and didn't get better. So when he came out of the forces he was by himself except for his family of course. Don't think me barmy but I do say my prayers and say thanks he came out of the war safely especially as he was torpedoed! Altho the Russians haven't a good name, they're very cruel to the Jewish people. I'm glad they were around to save him from drowning.

It was fascinating to hear about the people with whom you work but insurance?? How can you bear it after being in the midst of colour, thrills, dynamic goings on and everything that goes with film production and distribution!

Now I'm feeling sad at the thought of you and Belle being so far away. She also wanted to know what I had planned for my wedding PG but I know deep down the two of you aren't feeling excited for me. For a start there will be no Synagogue or Chupah. Mark won't break the glass and everyone shout out Muzzeltov! I find myself asking, well is all that really important, and the trouble is I feel I am missing out, and even more important is that I am taking away all the joy from my Mum and Dad and I can't bear the fact that they are so heartbroken. Sorry to be such a misery-guts, write and tell me what you and the new man are up to, and more about the Jewish community. Mum and Dad are interested and actually think your family have been very brave to make such a move. Are the streets and houses like ours over here?

Take care, lots of love

Lyn

Melody House.

Hi there dear Belle,

Wondering how you are all getting on. Hope Daddy is helping you take care of his precious daughter and Sharon is giving you some quiet nights. It looks as if I am never going to have such problems because the man I want to be the father of my children has called it a day. After all the chaos and heartache over Mum and Dad learning about Mark and thinking we'd worked things out I didn't reckon on more trouble. How wrong could I be!

One evening after work we went for a drink – have I told you this place isn't far from Wardour Street so Mark picks me up – and it seemed everything was great. I felt so happy! But guilt stirred when Mark said how sorry he was that Mum and Dad remained upset. "Parents have a great responsibility", he said softly and then took hold of my hand and squeezed it gently. "But I hope we can look forward to making the right moves when we have a family."

I know I write captions and letters easily but I can't find the words now to describe the joy which swept over me. But! I felt it was only fair to tell him what having a baby brings with it in our religion. I felt my cheeks burn as I told him boys had to be circumcised. Mark shrugged and said that was o.k., his Mother had approved of circumcision. So that was one good answer I'd hoped for, mind you I haven't a clue what difference there is between having and not having a circumcision. Perhaps as a long time wife you'll tell me one day!

Anyway, I told him, "It's called a Briss and a Rabbi has to see to the baby." He wanted to know why a doctor couldn't do it. I told him Jewish boys had to have a Rabbi.

Oh Belle, he went all stony cold, dropped my hand. "You seem to have taken it for granted that our babies are going to be Jewish."

I told him that was because the children of a Jewish mother are automatically Jewish. "Who says so?" he asked. I told him I didn't know, but that is how it's always been.

And he says, wait for it ... "But my Father will expect the child of his eldest son to follow in his footsteps and be baptised. My parents were wardens of their church ..."

Oh no no no, I pleaded silently to whoever is up there listening. I managed to croak out, "I can't help that. I'm Jewish and my children will be Jewish." Mark said, "But they won't just be your children, they'll be our children."

So the marvellous thought of having a family which should have given us such pleasure was now a thunderous shadow over us. I wiped my eyes – yes I'd started to blub – and blew my nose and took back his hand, lifted it against my cheek and said with as much lightness as possible in the circumstances, "Oh well there's only one thing for it no babies at all." He pulled his hand away and sat there unsmiling. "Now you're being foolish. In the circumstances we can't discuss this subject anymore - not the right time or place ..."

We walked to the car silently. No not silently, I was crying and blowing my nose. When was it going to be the right time or place? He drove me home, the radio was playng, he didn't speak. When we reached the house he came round and opened my door. I thought he would hug me and tell me not to worry, we'll fix it. But it was just a brief kiss on the cheek, no passion. Before he got back into the car he said it would be sensible to take our time to work things out. "I'll phone you if there is something to suggest."

I could hear Mum and Dad in the front room, they were with Connie and Stanley. I couldn't face them so went straight up. Connie must have heard me because she came rushing into the room, saw the state of me, there was no sympathy from her, if anything she was pleased that something had obviously gone wrong. "I could have told you ..." she began but stopped because I almost leapt on her ready to scratch her eyes out. That was about six weeks ago, each day I've gone to work and come home, no phone call. Mum and Dad have said nothing but I know they are pleased and that makes me ... this will sound wicked ... but I can't help it, I almost hate them. No I don't. I love them lots, but it hurts, I'm used to Mum cuddling me, making things better. I've thought about phoning Mark but I don't think I could hear him without crying again. And supposing he's cold or says he doesn't want to speak to me. I couldn't bear it.

Well Belle, any sympathy and advice for me? Supposing it was Sharon all grown up, kerhana hora, coming to you for help, what would you say?

Guess what Mum's just come in with a letter, it came yesterday and she wasn't going to give it to me but thought that would make things worse between us. I've read the letter, Mark's handwriting is beautiful but the contents have broken my heart. If we have a son PG, he could be circumcised by a Rabbi or whoever but he'd also be baptized. You're probably thinking the same as everyone else. I've made a big mistake which can't be rectified unless he accepts my Jewishness. So that's it.

Big hugs and kisses for Sharon.

Lyn.

Regency Close.

Darling Mark, what are we going to do? I can't believe that during our time together you haven't learnt what my religion means to me. There is no way a Jewish baby can or should be baptized, but don't think me selfish because it isn't that I intend to keep our children from knowing all about your religion. We'll see that they know about us both, what we believe and how we feel. We can even go to church together. The only difference between us would be that we wouldn't kneel down. Can't we meet and talk about everything? I can't bear the thought of not seeing you again, please please phone. I love you so much.

Lyn.

Please phone or pick me up at work. I miss you so much. You don't really want us to part do you?

Love

GLOSSARY

Barmitzvah	Jewish coming of age ritual
Briss	Jewish rite of circumcision, performed on a male child on the eight day of his life
Broigus	Trouble, argumentative
Buba	Grandmother
Chanukah	Jewish festival of rededication, also known as Festival of Lights
Chooch	Sweet man
Creeping Jesus	Unpleasantly insincere, untrustworthy or complaining person. (This strange expression distaste is mainly heard among middle-class speakers in Britain and Australia; it dates, according to the *Oxford English Dictionary*, at least to 1818.)
Gelt	Money
Gonif	Thief, tricky clever person, shady character
Goy	Non-Jew, Gentile
Haggadah	Text setting out the order of Passover Seder
Hemeshe	Homely
J.C.	Jewish Chronicle
Kamiah	Necklace with Star of David pendant
Kerhana hora	Blessing against the evil eye
Latkes and cucumbers	Potato pancakes and pickled gherkins
Magen David	Star of David
Ma Nishtana	One of the questions sung during the Passover Seder
Matzos	Unleavened bread traditionally eaten during Passover
M.D.A. Committee	Israeli Red Cross
Megillah	Long, complicated and boring
Mensch	Person of character
Meshuga	Crazy
Mitzvah	A commandment, but usually refers to a charitable, beneficial act
Muzick	Mischievous

Muzzeltov	Congratulations
Oi vey	"Oh, how terrible things are!"
Pesach	Passover
Rosh Hashana	Jewish New Year
Schidachs	Marriages
Schiddach-maker	Marriage broker
Schmattes	Rags or cloths
Schtum	Say nothing – especially in circumstances where saying the wrong thing may get you into trouble
Seder Night	Service observed on first night of Passover
Shabbas	Jewish Sabbath i.e. Saturday
Shema	A prayer that serves as a centerpiece of the morning and evening Jewish prayer services
Shiva	Week-long mourning period in Judaism for first-degree relatives
Shtook	Trouble
Shul	Synagogue
Tookus	Backside
Yid	Derogatory term
Yoks	Non-Jewish boys or men
Yom Kippur	Day of Atonement, the holiest day of the year for the Jewish people
Yomtov	Jewish holiday on which work is forbidden

Campaign

Friday August 20 1954

Golden Realm Marriage

Wardour Street turned out in their dozens, from film company Golden Realm, to celebrate the marriage of Mark Butler to his assistant Marilyn Ash. The wedding ceremony took place at Caxton Hall, Westminster.

Rer
foll
imp

The

Lightning Source UK Ltd.
Milton Keynes UK
UKOW06f0658081016

284772UK00013B/120/P

Ancient I

by James Mason

Contents

 LONGMAN

The land of Egypt

Egypt is in Africa. Thousands of years ago, in ancient times, it was very like it is today. It is a very hot country. Most of it is sandy desert where nothing grows. The only place where things grow is beside the River Nile which flows right through Egypt.

The bank of the River Nile today, with the desert beyond.

2

The Egyptians travelled by boat.
This model is over three thousand years old.

Every year for thousands of years the
Nile flooded its banks in the summer.
When the flood went down it left behind
a rich black mud in which people could
grow crops. They called their country
'the gift of the Nile' because the river
made it possible for them to live there.

3

How do we know?

We can find out about the ancient Egyptians from the clues they left behind. Some of the buildings and statues are still standing today. The buildings below are pyramids. Egyptian rulers had their bodies buried in tombs inside the pyramids when they died.

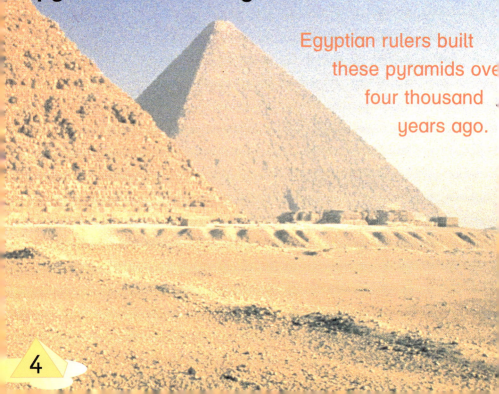

Egyptian rulers built these pyramids over four thousand years ago.

4

Archaeologists find out about the past from clues buried under the ground. The dry desert sand of Egypt holds many clues because it stops things from rotting. This is a painting from a nobleman's tomb. It shows him hunting.

Rulers and people

The pharaoh

The ruler, or pharaoh, of Egypt was the richest and most powerful person in the land. The people believed he was a god. They also expected him to keep Egypt safe from its enemies. There were some women pharaohs, but most were men.

This gold mask of Tutankhamun shows the headdress of a pharaoh.

Vulture god

Cobra goddess

Royal headcloth

Ceremonial beard

The vizir

The pharaoh appointed a vizir, or chief minister, to help him rule. The vizir organised the government and made sure the nobles in charge of different parts of the country did their jobs properly. He was also the chief judge.

People from other lands conquered by the Egyptians bring gifts to the vizir.

Scribes

The Egyptians were one of the first peoples to invent writing. Egyptians who could write were called scribes. Scribes were important people. Many of them worked in the pharaoh's royal palace or as government officials.

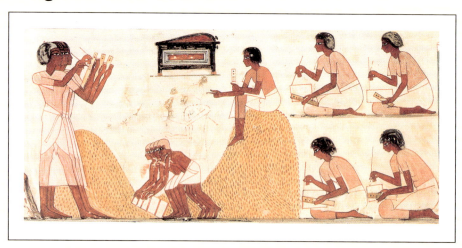

Scribes writing down how much corn has been harvested from the pharaoh's fields. Can you see their brushes and brush boxes with two holes for dried paint?

Picture writing from the wall of a tomb.

At first the Egyptians used picture writing.
Some pictures stood for whole words.
Some stood for sounds, like our letters.

Then they invented a new, quicker, way
of writing. Scribes used a brush made
from a thin reed split at one end. They
wrote on a kind of paper, called

papyrus, also made
from reeds.

The new writing on
a piece of papyrus.

Craftworkers

Many Egyptians earned their living by working at a skilled craft. There were builders, stoneworkers, carpenters, metal workers and people who made fine jewellery from precious metals such as gold and silver.

This painting shows a carpenter at work. He is using a tool called an adze to smooth the surface of the wood.

The picture on the back of the throne shows Tutankhamun with his wife, Queen Ankesenamun.

Some of the most skilful workers made things for the pharaoh in the workshops of the royal palace. This is a throne made for the pharaoh, Tutankhamun.

Farmers

Egyptian farmers had to provide enough food for their own families and for all the people who did other jobs. This tomb painting shows farmers at work after the River Nile's summer flood. A few months later they harvested their crops.

Hoeing

Sowing seeds

Breaking up lumps of soil

Ploughing

Servants and slaves

Thousands of Egyptians worked on the land for the pharaoh and other rich people. Thousands of other men and women were paid to work as servants in people's houses. Some people were slaves, which meant they had to work for their owner and could be bought and sold.

A model of a servant carrying bread and meat.

13

The home

More than three thousand years ago a pharaoh decided he wanted his dead body to be buried in a secret tomb in a desert valley. Other pharaohs followed his example. Archaeologists have found the remains of the village where the tomb-builders and their families lived.

The tomb-builders' village.
Archaeologists found many clues about the lives of ordinary Egyptians here.

14

This is what archaeologists think the tomb-builders' houses were like.

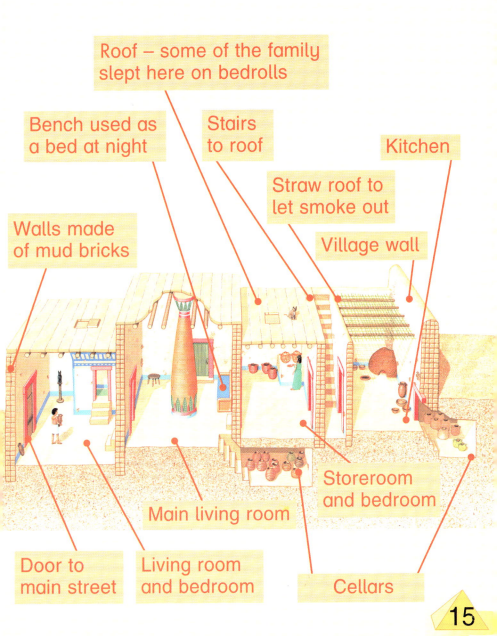

Roof – some of the family slept here on bedrolls

Bench used as a bed at night

Stairs to roof

Kitchen

Straw roof to let smoke out

Walls made of mud bricks

Village wall

Storeroom and bedroom

Main living room

Door to main street

Living room and bedroom

Cellars

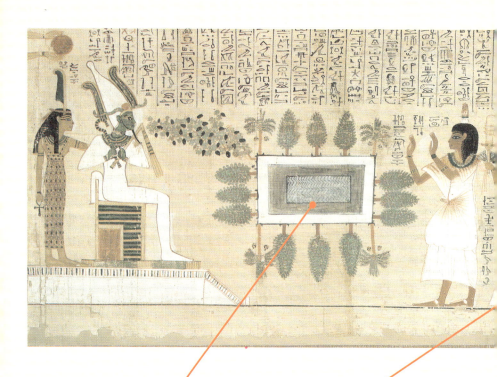

Pond

Date palm tree

Fruit tree

Ramp to keep out floodwater and damp

This painting shows a scribe and his wife worshipping the god Osiris, the god of the dead. It gives us clues about the houses and gardens of rich people.

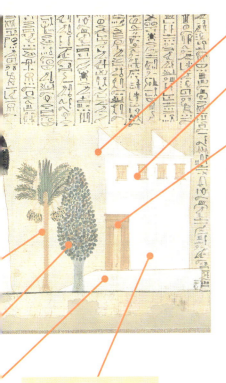

Opening for air

Small windows to let in light but keep out the sun

Door

Mudbrick walls covered in white plaster

This collection of furniture includes a three-legged table, a decorated wine jar and a finely made stool and chair.

Poor Egyptians had very little furniture in their houses. The most common items were small three-legged stools. Better-off people had simple but well-made stools, tables, chests and beds as well as various decorated pots.

The family

The Egyptians married when they were quite young. Parents sometimes arranged their children's marriages, but most couples probably chose each other. Couples were allowed to divorce. If they did so, they shared their property.

A statue of a worker and his wife from the tomb-builder's village. They have their arms around each other.

A toy lion with moveable jaws.

A wooden doll with
moveable arms.

All couples wanted to have children,
but many babies died from illnesses.
Even so, families were often large.
Children kept pets, played ball games
and owned toys.

These two quarrelling girls have been sent to collect up any corn left on the ground after harvesting.

In many households, children had to help with the work. Most children were brought up to do the same jobs as their parents. Men usually worked outside the home while women worked in it; but many women did extra jobs, for example as weavers or musicians.

Dress

The Egyptians grew a crop called flax.
They took the stringy bits, or fibres,
from its stem and spun them into thread.
Then they wove the threads into a cloth
called linen. They made all their clothes
from linen.

On their feet they
wore sandals
made from reeds.

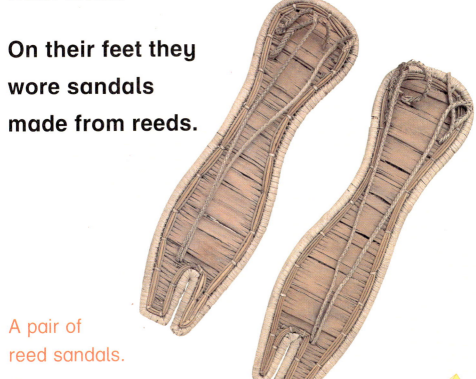

A pair of
reed sandals.

In earliest times Egyptian men wore short kilts and women wore long, plain dresses held up by shoulder straps. This family is wearing the fashions that came in later.

Wigs

Robe with pleats and fringes worn over a dress

Long curling piece of hair to show the child is not yet grown up

Long kilt

On important occasions wealthy adults wore wigs over their short hair. Both men and women wore make-up and jewellery. They put green or grey paint around their eyes, partly to look good and partly to protect their skin from the sun.

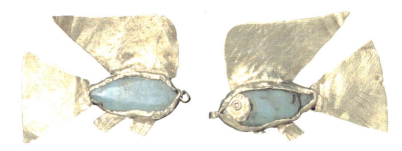

Young girls wore fish like these in their hair as charms to prevent them from drowning.

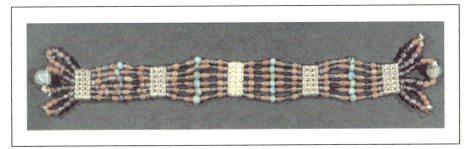

A bracelet.

Food

All Egyptians ate bread and fish, but only the better-off could afford meat or birds such as ducks and geese. The Egyptians made wine from grapes, but the most popular drink for ordinary people was beer made from barley.

Treading grapes to squeeze out the juice to make wine.

The Egyptians grew all sorts of fruit and vegetables in their fields and gardens. Here are some other foods that they enjoyed eating.

Figs

Dates

Lettuce

Lentils

Pomegranates

Broad beans

Honey

Cucumber

Onion

Entertainment

Wealthy Egyptians gave parties with lots of food and drink, called banquets. Servants put garlands of flowers round the guests' necks and blocks of scent on top of their wigs. The scent melted and ran down their bodies.

Musicians and dancers performing at a banquet. The musicians are wearing blocks of scent.

All Egyptians loved feasting, dancing, acrobatics, singing and music. Their instruments included flutes, harps, castanets and drums. They also played board games such as draughts. Their favourite game was called 'senet', but we do not know the rules.

The gods

The Egyptians worshipped many gods and goddesses. The pharaohs had special buildings called temples built for them. People believed the gods lived there in the form of statues. Priests looked after the statues and gave them offerings of food and drink.

Modern visitors looking at the remains of a temple built for the chief god, Amun-Re.

Gods and goddesses took various shapes: human, animal or a mixture. The god Bes was partly human, partly a lion. His job was to bring happiness to the home. Many families prayed to him and kept his statue in their house.

The god Bes playing a tambourine.

29

The afterlife

The Egyptians believed that after death they would lead a new, happy life in the underworld, so they thought it was important that dead bodies should not rot. They used special ointments and wax to preserve them. Preserved bodies are called mummies.

This wooden case holds the mummy of a woman priest. The painted lid shows what she might have looked like.

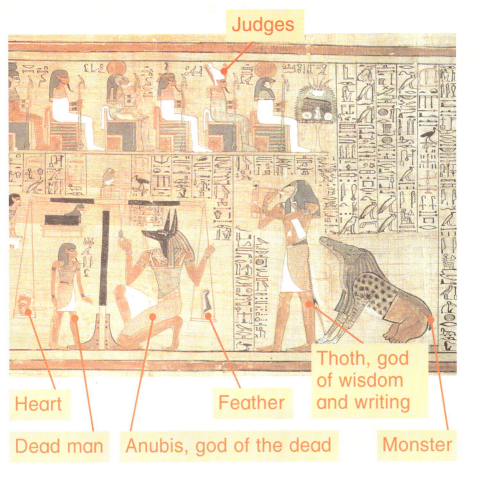

Judges

Heart

Thoth, god of wisdom and writing

Feather

Dead man

Anubis, god of the dead

Monster

This dead man has reached the underworld. Now he has to prove he has led a good life. His heart is weighed against a feather. If it is heavier than the feather, he is wicked and a monster will eat him. If it is lighter, he may go in.

Index